Volume Two

AIRSHIP 27 PRODUCTIONS

The Moon Man Volume 2

"Silver Trail" © 2018 Gene Moyers
"Moon Boys" © 2018 Greg Hatcher
"The Faceless Terror" © 2018 Tim Holter Bruckner
"Invasion: Great City" © 2018 Terry Alexander

Interior illustrations © 2018 Richard Jun
Cover illustration © 2018 Mike Fyles

Editor: Ron Fortier
Associate Editor: Jonathan Sweet
Production and design by Rob Davis
Promotion and marketing by Michael Vance

Published by
Airship 27 Productions
www.airship27.com
www.airship27hangar.com

ISBN-13: 978-1-946183-35-4
ISBN-10: 1-946183-35-0

Printed in the United States of America

10 9 8 7 6 5 4 3 2 1

VOLUME TWO
CONTENTS

SILVER TRAIL
By Gene Moyers

The room was in total darkness. The only sound came from the ticking of a clock hanging on the darkened wall. This near silence was broken by the metallic clicking of a lock clicking back. A door opened and the figure of a tall well-built man was momentarily silhouetted against the light before he slipped through the door and it closed behind him. The darkness was then pierced by the narrow beam of a pencil flashlight. The flash revealed a well-furnished living room. The beam moved around and steadied on a doorway. Once inside this room the flashlight revealed an expensively furnished study. Books lined one wall while a large oak desk and comfortable leather chair dominated the center of the room. The light clicked off and a shadowy figure moved to the window, drawing the heavy drapes. The nearly invisible figure glided to the desk and there was a scrabbling sound as hands moved over its surface. A click was followed by the shaded light of a green desk light brightening the area. The dim light barely illuminated the desk and a few feet around it. The light could not be seen outside the room. The burglar bent over the desk. Using a small skeleton key he quickly manipulated the lock in the center drawer that unlocked all the other drawers. Reaching for the lowest drawer on the right side of the desk he opened it and quickly removed all the files and assorted paperwork within. Removing his glove he felt carefully around until he found a narrow slit into which he inserted his fingernail. Pulling, he lifted out the false bottom that revealed a wide flat compartment two inches deep. The beam of the flashlight showed only one item concealed in the hidden compartment; an eight by ten inch professional style ledger an inch thick. Removing his remaining glove, the burglar took the ledger and laid it on the desk. Opening it, he paged through it until he found the page he was looking for. Settling himself in the chair behind the desk, he fished a pen from his coat pocket and began copying information from the ledger onto loose sheets of paper he had also pulled from his pocket.

There was much information to copy. Columns of names, dates and money amounts filled the books. There were also addresses, dates and times listed. The burglar worked silently and steadily. He had spent weeks to locate this book. The man who lived in this apartment was the chief accountant for the notorious Baker mob. Baker's gang had plagued Great

City for years. They controlled much of the gambling, prostitution and loan sharking in the city and were responsible for corruption amongst many normally honest citizens. The data the burglar was copying from the ledger would be enough to crush the Baker mob, but he had other ideas for how to use the information. Before the Baker mob could be brought down he intended to return some of their ill-gotten gains to a needy public.

He had been working for over an hour when the telephone on the desk rang. The burglar froze with his fountain pen pressed to the paper. The phone rang only once and was silent. The burglar counted silently to himself. At the count of ten the phone rang again. He lifted the receiver and spoke, "Yes."

"Duling is leaving the restaurant. They're bringing his car around now. If he drives straight home he'll be there in fifteen minutes. He might be headed elsewhere but I wouldn't count on it. You better get out of there, Boss."

"I'm leaving now, Angel," he said and then quietly cradled the receiver. Thoughtfully he continued writing, more quickly now. Soon he glanced at his watch; time to go. Standing, he quickly replaced the ledger in its hidden compartment. He then replaced all the paperwork in the drawer and closed it. He relocked the desk and looked carefully around. He made some small adjustment to items on the desk until it was as he remembered. He then clicked off the light and moved to the window where he opened the drapes. Moving carefully he exited the study and closed the door behind him. He clicked on the flashlight momentarily to glide across to the front door of the apartment. There he clicked it off and put his ear to the front door. Hearing nothing, he opened the door and looked both ways at an empty corridor. Slipping out, it was but a second's work to relock the door. The burglar then strode briskly to the stair well and down to the lobby. He crossed it casually and exited onto the street without incident. As he strolled down the street he glanced at his watch. Twelve minutes. He smiled to himself.

A few blocks later he hailed a cab and gave the driver directions. He got out in front of an apartment building. Stopping at a newsstand that was just closing, he put a nickel on the counter and picked up a newspaper from a stack. The friendly newsie smiled and asked, "Is that it for you tonight, Sergeant?"

As he turned to enter the apartment building, Detective Steve Thatcher of the Great City police force nodded. "That's all for tonight. Good night, Frank."

The man carrying the briefcase hesitated at the mouth of the alley. He could see the idling car waiting for him directly across the street. He could see the driver's silhouette behind the wheel. He glanced left and right. The dimly lit street was deserted at this late hour. Reassured, he started across the street. He passed in front of the sedan and reached for the passenger door handle. As he swung the door wide he felt a sharp prod in the small of his back and a loud, oddly hollow whisper in his ear, "I'll take that case." He froze for a moment waiting but his driver remained motionless behind the wheel. Another prod, this time accompanied by the ominous double click of a handgun being thumbed back to full cock. "Just hand it back slowly."

Reaching back with his right arm, he was quickly relieved of the briefcase's heavy weight.

"Now, get in the car and close the door."

The former courier got into the sedan and closed the door with an angry slam. He glanced quickly to his left. The driver was unconscious, his head lolled back on the seat. His jacket had been wrenched open and his shoulder holster was empty. Looking back quickly to his right he saw a bizarre figure retreating down a dark alley. This figure was dressed in some kind of long black robe that was now merging with the darkness of the alley. The only thing about the fellow that stood out in the darkness was a silver globe atop his shoulders that quickly was becoming smaller until it too was swallowed by the blackness. Sitting there in the car, the courier was relieved. He wouldn't have to explain to his certain-to-be-furious boss about being robbed by a street hood. He had been robbed by the notorious Moon Man.

The silver globed figure paused cautiously for a moment at the mouth of the alley. A powerful roadster idled at the curb, the rest of the block seemed deserted. Quickly he entered the roadster. The stocky driver put the car into gear and drove quietly away. Keeping his eyes on the road he inquired, "Everything go okay, Boss?"

"Just fine Angel." He patted the heavy briefcase on his lap. "I'm sure there's plenty here to help a lot of people. It looks like the information we worked so hard for is paying off." Reaching up the Moon Man removed the silver globe that covered his head, pulled off his black gloves and slipped out of his long black robe. Uncoupling the two halves of his helmet, Detective Steve Hatcher stuffed his disguise into a small overnight case which he stowed on the floor of the car.

As the roadster powered quietly through the city streets, Steve reflected on the evening's encounter. The courier had been on time and everything had gone perfectly. It looked as if his new strategy was working. Recently, a major break had fallen his way. It had taken weeks of work but he had finally discovered the identity and location of the chief accountant for the vicious Baker gang. A few nights earlier he had burgled the apartment of the bookkeeper. There he had discovered complete records of all Baker's activities. They were so detailed he was forced to go back a second time to complete transcribing the incriminating information. Steve had been torn at that point. He could easily have sent those records anonymously to the police who would have completely smashed Baker's mob; putting them all behind bars for many years. On the other hand, with the records he had found, he could observe Baker's activities and make a series of targeted strikes against the mobster's many illegal operations; easily gaining tens of thousands of dollars. This would insure a steady stream of income that would help many people who had been victimized by the terrible economic times. The best part was that these activities would all be low profile strikes that would go unseen by the authorities. The Baker mob would certainly not complain to the police. With no seeming activity by their nemesis, the police, especially the bulldog Lt. Gil McEwen, might scale back their pursuit of the Moon Man for a while. A pleasant thought, if it worked out.

Passing through a run-down section of town they pulled up in front of an abandoned tenement. Getting out of the car, Steve locked the case containing his disguise in the roadster's rumble seat. His driver had also gotten out of the car. "Angel," actually Ned Dargan, former prize fighter, was short and strongly built. In the dark you could hardly see his cauliflower ear or that his nose had been broken several times. He was not the most handsome man in the world but Steve knew he was loyal to a fault. Steve had rescued him from a desperate situation and now Ned was his loyal aide and confidant. In addition he was one of only two people in the world who knew that Steve Hatcher was actually the notorious Moon Man.

Handing over the briefcase Steve asked, "I'm sure there is enough here to help out more than a few people. Do you have some needy candidates in mind?"

"You bet. I've got a list of dozens of hurting families; most out of work, a lot of them in danger of being put out on the streets."

"Good. Take this and see what you can do with it. I'll be in touch soon."

Angel held out his hand and Steve shook it firmly, "Take care Boss." Then Angel turned and made his way up the steps and into the darkened building. Steve slipped behind the wheel of the car and put it in gear. No one saw the powerful roadster purr away into the darkness.

A half hour later, the handsome brown haired figure of Steve Thatcher entered an Italian restaurant. He spoke to the hostess and was quickly shown to the table of a beautiful young woman with light brown hair and a shy smile. She stood up as he approached and he embraced her with a light kiss to her lips. He held her at arm's length for a moment gazing lovingly at Sue McEwen, his fiancé and only daughter of his boss, Lt Gil McEwen; ace detective of the Great City police force. She and Ned Dargan were the only people in the world who knew that the Moon Man was in reality Detective Sergeant Steve Hatcher, son of the respected police chief Peter Hatcher.

Sue frowned through her smile. "Steve, you're late. I was worried."

As he seated himself, Steve smiled at his fiancé."Nothing to worry about, just running a little behind schedule."

"But you know how I worry whenever you're out there. . ." She looked carefully around and dropped her voice to a whisper, "…as the Moon Man. Was there any trouble?"

Picking up a menu, Steve shook his head and smiled. "Not really. I had to wait longer than I thought for my 'appointment' but it went well after that."

Sue looked at Steve sadly. "I know you do so much good and have helped so many people Steve, but I can't help thinking what will happen if you're caught. It will mean ruin and prison; the end of your life and mine too, because my life is nothing without you." Steve smiled bravely but couldn't help thinking of the other damage that would be done if he was exposed as the mysterious Moon Man. It would be a terrible blow to his aging father and to Sue's father Gil. Their careers would likely be over as well, for public opinion would no doubt drive them into retirement.

He waved the waitress over to order some wine and smiled, "Things may get easier for a while."

"Oh I hope so. I see so little of you and worry so much."

Steve took her hand and was going to say more but at that moment their wine arrived and they got busy ordering their late dinner. They avoided controversial topics through the rest of the evening. Instead they chatted about their daily affairs. Sue was especially excited about some of the plans for their future wedding. On the way home they held hands but were quiet, content with the time that they had had together. Steve eventually pulled his car into the driveway of a modest home in an established residential neighborhood. The house was dark except for a light in the downstairs living room. Steve walked Sue up to the porch where she opened the door with her key. As the two entered the comfortably furnished living room a man stood up from the sofa. He was a fit, fiftyish man with gray eyes that peered from a tough, weathered face tanned like old leather. He had a sheaf of papers in one hand as he greeted the young people, "Steve, Sue, back so soon? What time is it?"

Sue wagged a finger at her father. "Soon? Dad, it's late. What are you still doing up?"

Surprised, Gil McEwen glanced at his wrist watch. "Uh, I was just doing some paperwork and lost track of time."

"And just what was so important that you're working on it when you should be in bed?"

McEwen hesitated as if at a loss for words. Sue smiled and inquired innocently, "It wouldn't have anything to do with the Moon Man would it?" McEwen looked surprised but before he could answer Sue spoke again. "Oh Dad, you're not working on another hair brained scheme to trap him again, are you?"

McEwen bristled. "By damn! It's my duty to put that menace away. He's the only crook that's ever escaped me and I will see him fry for his crimes if it's the last thing I do. And just why are you defending him young lady?"

Feisty Sue fired right back at her gruff father. "You know very well that if it wasn't for the Moon Man I would be in jail right this minute for murder. He's the one who proved me innocent. I'd think you would remember that!"

"I remember, and I still don't get it. But that's neither here nor there. He's still a criminal and it's our duty to put him away. Isn't that right Steve?" A little out of his depth Gil looked hopefully to Steve for support.

Steve smiled and shook his head. "I believe in duty Gil, but I've got to side with Sue on this one. Without the Moon Man I'd be visiting my fiancé at the state prison and you'd never be walking her down the aisle to me. Maybe the Moon Man isn't as bad as we all think."

"Oh, he's a crook alright. And I'll get him. Maybe sooner than he thinks if my new plan works."

Very interested now, Steve inquired casually, "Oh, something in the works, eh? What is it?"

McEwen waved he papers negligently, "Not tonight it's late. When I've got all the details worked out I'll bring you in. You'll have a big enough part in it Steve."

Steve nodded, if there were a plot to catch the Moon Man he would have a part in it, of that he was sure. He kissed Sue goodnight and told Gil he would see him at headquarters the next day. He then drove away wondering what Gil had come up with this time to catch his wily opponent.

Steve exchanged greetings with other officers as he entered police headquarters the next morning. He checked his mail slot and then briskly made his way upstairs to the office of the police chief. Knocking once, he entered to have his father, Peter Thatcher, long time police chief of Great City, smile at him. "Good morning Son."

"Morning Dad, Gil," he greeted, acknowledging McEwen's presence.

The hard-eyed McEwen monetarily stopped his pacing to greet Steve. "Hello, Steve."

"You look serious Gil. What's going on?"

Gil pointed at Chief Thatcher. "The chief and I were just speculating on why we haven't heard from the Moon Man lately. He thinks the man may be lying low for a while."

Steve watched McEwen closely. "And what do you think Gil?"

Gilbert McEwen was the hard driving ace of the detective division of the Great City police force. He prided himself on never having had a crook escape him. The one exception had become his obsession: The Moon Man. Gil glared at Steve, "Oh he's still around, and he's not lying low. He's busy, by damn! Busy planning his next crime, and when he does I'll be there!" He suddenly stopped speaking and grinned slyly. "But maybe we won't have to wait for whatever dastardly plot he's got brewing. Maybe we'll make him come to us."

"I don't know? Dad may be right. Could be he's got plenty of loot and is taking it easy. We may not hear from him for some time. He might even be out of town now."

McEwen shot Steve a cunning look. "If he's out of town, I've got just the thing to draw him back. Every trap just needs the right bait." He smiled thinly.

Steve kept a calm look on his face. His worst nightmare was that someday Gil McEwen would unmask him; expose him as the Moon Man. It would mean the end of everything. The knowledge would crush his father not to mention Gil himself. And when he found out that his own daughter had known the Moon Man's identity all along; the consequences were too terrible to even consider. And now it sounded like Gil was planning another trap for the Moon Man. He tried to look casually interested. "So, what have you got planned Gil? Whatever it is, you know you can count on me."

Gil absently nodded. "Sure Steve, when the time comes you'll be in on the kill."

Steve probed gently. "Something soon?"

Gil rubbed his hands together rather gleefully. "Soon enough if my plan works out."

Chief Thatcher spoke up. "Don't keep us in suspense Gil. What's your new plan?"

Gil looked slightly uncomfortable as he spoke respectfully to the chief. "I'd rather not say right now. I've still got to get the cooperation of a few key people. But things could be ready fairly soon."

Steve asked a couple more questions but it was apparent that McEwen was playing his cards pretty close to the vest on this latest scheme. Making his excuses, Steve returned to his desk to work on paperwork and brood on what McEwen was up to.

The next night Steve was waiting at the mouth of an alley on a deserted street. There were only a few cars on the street. He clutched a small overnight case in one hand. The other gripped his revolver in his overcoat pocket. Eventually a roadster turned onto the street and drove slowly past. As it passed the mouth of the alley, Steve recognized it and stepped out. The car eased to a stop and Steve slipped quickly into the passenger seat. The driver let in the clutch and the powerful car purred away. "Hello Boss, good to see you."

"Good to see you too, Angel. Ready for a big night?"

Ned Dargan glanced quickly at the young detective who had saved him from oblivion and for whom he would gladly give his life, "You bet, Boss. There are lots of people out there who need our help. For that, I'm always ready."

Steve nodded. He glanced at his watch. "If Baker's courier is on time he

"Good to see you too, Angel. Ready for a big night?"

should be picking up today's take from his pleasure house on Park Street soon. We'll see if we can pick him up there. Ned grinned and powered the roadster through the nearly empty streets.

Five minutes later Angel pulled over and eased the car to a stop at the corner of Park and Atlantic streets. He killed the lights and gently eased the car forward enough so the two of them could look past the corner building down Park Street. A few lights were on in buildings but there was little foot traffic and the only illumination came from scattered street lights. Most buildings were dark but halfway down the street a four story building was well lit with lights in many of its front windows. As they watched, two men came out of the front door and made their way to a parked car and drove away. Directly in front of the building a sedan idled. Its exhaust trailed condensation in the cool night air. Steve could clearly see the silhouettes of two men sitting in the automobile. Then a figure stepped out of the front door but hesitated at the top of the steps leading to the sidewalk. Immediately, a large bulky man stepped out of the sedan. Looking slowly around, the man waved to the fellow on the steps as he opened a rear door of the car. The man then hurried down the steps and into the back of the sedan. He carried what appeared to be a large briefcase. The large man got back in the front seat and the sedan drove down the street.

"Okay Angel, stay with them. No lights."

"Right, Boss."

Angel turned the darkened roadster after the sedan. As they followed it through the deserted streets Steve observed, "Looks like the driver has picked up a friend."

Angel chuckled. "Guess they're worried Boss, think we can handle an extra one?"

"I think we can find a way to convince them to contribute to our worthy cause." Angel laughed. They followed the car to its next destination. They waited well back as it made another stop. The man with the briefcase got out and entered an alley. The large bulky man exited the sedan and waited at the alley mouth until the briefcase carrying man returned and they both got in the car. It then moved quietly off down the street.

Steve looked at his watch again. "Alright Angel, it's time to make our move. Their next pick up should be on Spruce, off 35th. Turn right at the next corner and open it up. We need to get there ahead of them." Angel nodded and pressed down on the accelerator as the roadster shot forward.

Streaking through the streets, sometimes with lights and sometimes without, Angel managed to reach their destination in just minutes. They turned onto Spruce and Steve pointed to an empty stretch of curb. "Pull in there. You know what to do." As Angel wheeled the car to the curb, Steve opened up the overnight case. He pulled out a long black robe that he quickly threw over his shoulders. He then pulled out the two silvery half globes made of rare Argus glass, hooked them together and quickly placed them over his head. Angel got out of the car and trotted up several steps to the doorway of a brownstone building. With the silvery globe on his head obscuring his features, the Moon Man pulled on a pair of thin black gloves and reached for the last item in the case, a large automatic pistol. Working the slide, he chambered a round and slipped it into an opening in his robe. He looked at the brownstone but could not see Angel concealed in the dark doorway. He looked over his shoulder through the rear window of the roadster just in time to see a pair of headlights turn into the block. Gripping his concealed pistol, the Moon Man sank down in his seat below window level so that the roadster appeared empty to the approaching vehicle. Without having to look, the Moon Man knew that the sedan would pull up directly in front of the building that was the collecting point for numbers runners from across the city. That put the idling auto approximately thirty feet behind the parked roadster; now it was up to Angel.

From the darkened doorway Angel saw the larger car coast to a stop and the courier exit carrying his briefcase. He waited, counting under his breath. Steve had said timing here was very important. When he reached the proper moment, Angel took a deep breath and whistling a merry tune he clattered down the front steps toward the roadster. He rounded the front of the car and reached for the driver's door handle. He totally ignored the sedan and its occupants. Crouched down holding his gun, the Moon Man could hear Angel's nonchalant approach. He assumed the two gunmen in the sedan were watching Angel carefully. Angel opened the driver's door and cheerfully hopped in. Pressing the starter he engaged the gear shift while quietly mouthing, "They're still in the car Boss, they're buying it."

Revving the engine, Angel let in the clutch and the car lurched backwards; he had put it in reverse. The car darted backwards and crunched into the heavier sedan's bumper with a solid metallic whang! Taking the car out of gear, Angel opened his door and jumped out. Running to the rear of their car he exclaimed, "Oh no. I'm sorry mister; I sure didn't mean that to happen." From his place on the floor of the front seat, the Moon Man could hear car doors open and angry voices cursing loudly. It sounded as if both thugs were out of the car. One voice was shouting, "You mug! Look what you did! Where'd you learn how to drive?"

In a sincere voice Angel apologized. "Look, I musta got the wrong gear, I'm really. . ."

That was his cue. The Moon Man grabbed his door handle, shoved the door open and rolled out onto the sidewalk with his automatic up and pointed. The two Baker hoods were standing where the two cars bumpers met staring down at the damage. One was in the street just in front of Ned. The other was ten feet away from the Moon Man on the sidewalk. His gun coming level with the nearest thug's chest, the Moon Man barked, "Hands up! Don't go for those guns!"

Caught flat footed, the two shocked gunmen raised their hands. Having drawn his own gun, Angel moved forward quickly and disarmed his man, tossing the gun into the street. The Moon Man stood up and quickly took a gun from the hood in front of him. Quickly they ordered the two thugs to lie on the ground. The Moon Man then glided to the nearby doorway just in time to meet the courier carrying a heavy briefcase as he exited onto the sidewalk. Leveling his gun at the courier's face he quickly relieved him of the briefcase and ordered him to the ground next to his guards. The briefcase in one hand and his pistol in the other, the Moon Man walked backward to the roadster. Angel was already behind the wheel; the Moon Man took careful aim and put two bullets in to the sedan's radiator before jumping into their car. Angel let in the clutch and roared away.

When they were convinced there was no pursuit, Angel slowed the car to the speed limit while Steve removed his costume and stowed it in its case. He had Angel slow the car as they neared his apartment building. He got out but leaned back to speak quietly to Angel, "You know what to do, right Angel?"

"Right Boss. I've got list of people this stuff will help."

"Good. Work on that for a day or two, but be careful. I'll call you soon."

Angel waved and purred away in the powerful, souped-up car.

Arriving the next day at police headquarters, Steve checked his mail and then went looking for Gil McEwen. He was not at his desk but Steve finally located him in Chief Thatcher's office. He knocked and entered. As expected, Gil was pacing back and forth talking up his favorite subject; the Moon Man. He stopped as Steve entered. "Hello Steve, I was just telling your father a little bit about my new plan to lure that masked menace out of hiding. Maybe you have some thoughts on why we haven't heard from him lately?"

Steve was torn. What he really wanted to do was ask McEwen about this new plan but at the same time he didn't want to look too interested. Pasting a casual look on his face he shrugged. "Not sure Gil. Could be he's collected so much loot in the last few months he's decided to take a vacation." He accompanied this with a small smile and another shrug.

McEwen fumed. "Oh no; he's not on vacation. He's here and he hasn't changed his ways. He may be robbing crooks rather than honest folk but he'll never change. And I won't either. I don't care who he's stealing from. By damn, I've sworn to put him away and I won't rest until he fries!"

Recognizing that Gil was on one of his rants, Steve tried to calm him down. "I know you'll get him Gil. What's your new plan?"

"Well, it's a good one. I'll have everything in place soon. Just a couple more details to get straight. Then I'll bring everyone in on it."

Inside Steve was sweating but he smiled as he kidded Gil. "Come on Gil. What's the big secret? You've taken me into your confidence before. You don't think I'm working with the Moon Man, do you?"

Gil shook his head. "Of course not Steve. But I've been close before and every time I think I've got a fool proof plan to catch that masked menace he slips right through my fingers. I don't know how he does it but I'm taking no chances this time. I'm keeping everything to myself until the last minute. But don't you worry Steve; you'll be in on the kill. I'll see to that." Steve smiled ruefully to himself; if the Moon Man was to be trapped he would no doubt be there, one way or another.

The rest of the morning passed quickly with Steve at his desk doing paperwork but mostly worrying about what Gil was up to this time. Soon enough he was disturbed by the attractive figure of his fiancé, Sue McEwen, striding into the squad room. She strode directly to his desk unaware of the admiring looks given her by the other detectives. "Steve, I have orders directly from both the chief and the head of detectives that you are to take me to lunch. So no arguments, my car is outside."

Steve leaned back in his chair and spread his hands in surrender. "Well, orders are orders. I always follow them, it's my sworn duty." Grabbing his hat, he offered Sue his arm and escorted her to her car. A short trip across the business district brought them to one of their favorite restaurants. After they were seated and had ordered, Sue spoke. "Okay, why are you looking so serious? Did you have problems on your special job last night?"

Steve smiled. "No that came off just fine. No one hurt and plenty of goods for the cause, if you know what I mean."

"Well, what then?"

"Oh, it's your Dad. He's got another scheme up his sleeve to trap the Moon Man and I've been trying to pry it out of him."

"Oh Steve, you're probably worrying about nothing. He's done this before and you've always been able to avoid his traps."

"True, but it's only been because I've had previous knowledge of what he's been up to, and sometimes it's been a near run thing."

Sue put her hand over his and looked lovingly into his eyes. "Don't worry, Steve. I know you'll be fine."

He agreed. "I know I will, it's just that so much depends on keeping my secret. Not just my work for the poor but our life together. It would ruin us and everyone we love if I fail."

"Well, I'll do everything I can. Perhaps I can get father to give away some hints this evening. If I do, I'll let you know as soon as I can. What are your plans tonight? Can you come by the house?"

Steve sighed. "I wish I could but I have to do some reconnaissance tonight."

"Is it dangerous?'

"No, just watching and planning. I'll call you tomorrow and we'll talk." The rest of their lunch passed pleasantly and then Sue dropped Steve back at the station.

Several times during the rest of the afternoon Steve had conversations with McEwen. They discussed several aspects of their work but whenever Steve maneuvered the topic around to the Moon Man, Gil would become reticent and just smile. Finally quitting time came and Steve made a quick exit. Stopping at home, he ate and then changed into non-descript clothing before setting out to keep watch on Baker's collection courier. Since he had studied the accountant's notes carefully, he knew just where Baker's man would be during the evening and could plan accordingly.

The courier's first pick up for the evening was at an all-night drug store; a drop off point for various numbers runners and their gambling profits. Arriving there early, Steve parked his car around the corner and loitered in a darkened doorway. He watched the quiet street until a dark sedan pulled and parked in front of the drug store. Pulling his cap down low over his face, Steve stepped out and walked casually toward the store. As he neared, the two large men with their hands in their overcoat pockets gave him a good look over. Obviously his rough working clothes and casual manner passed inspection because they made no attempt to stop him from entering the drug store. As he opened the door a familiar figure carrying a briefcase brushed past him and ducked quickly into the waiting car. The two burly guards ducked in after him and the sedan pulled away. As they passed, Steve got a good look into their car. Just the two guards; no more than last time he thought to himself. He turned back onto the sidewalk to find his car when a second black sedan sped quickly down the street after the pick-up car.

Steve turned to look at this new car as it passed the lighted store. He quickly discerned four bulky figures in suits and overcoats. This was unexpected. The car full of men turned at the corner and followed after the first sedan. Surprised, Steve hesitated for a moment before sprinting for his own car. Using his knowledge of the gang's schedule and a bit of aggressive driving, he managed to get ahead of Baker's vehicle. Once more he pulled up across the street from an exclusive night spot. The club was legitimate but the gambling that took place in the spacious back rooms was not. Steve killed his engine and slumped down in the seat; his eyes just at window level. He had barely gotten into position when the mysterious sedan drove slowly past. It was the pursuing car Steve had first seen at the drug store. The big car turned into the block, pulled over at the corner and stopped. Its lights went out but no one emerged from it. A minute later a second car turned into the block and this one stopped directly in front of the night club. Two over-coated men got out and looked carefully around. Then a third figure exited the car and carrying a case entered the night club. Steve continued to watch and several minutes later the man with the case left the night club and re-entered his car. He and his body guards then quickly drove away. Steve watched curiously as the dark sedan full of men followed the first car. Sitting up, Steve thought things over. So, Baker had upped the ante. He now had a full car of gunmen following his pick-up man, just in case the Moon Man put in an appearance. This would take some re-thinking. He started his roadster and set off to the next destination of the courier's route. Steve continued this for another two hours. By the time he had seen the courier make all his pick-ups and return to Baker's headquarters, the beginnings of a plan had begun to form in his mind. It would take some careful planning but with Angel's help it could be done. He turned his car around and headed for home.

Before he could even get to his desk the next morning, he was waylaid by Gil McEwen. Taking him by the arm, the smiling McEwen guided him into Chief Thatcher's office and closed the door. Gil was practically beaming as he exclaimed, "Well everything is in place. My plan is underway. Now it's time to bring you into it."

The chief shook his head. "Well, it's high time Gil. You've been prowling around here for days keeping us all in suspense."

"Sorry chief, but I've been disappointed before. This time I wanted everything in place. That way there's less to go wrong. This time we're going to have the Moon Man trapped."

Looking interested, Steve took a seat and said, "Okay Gil, tell us about it."

Nodding, McEwen started in. "Firstly we need the right bait. We've come close to catching the Moon Man several times, and he's worried. I believe he's lying low waiting for something big. Only the right bait will tempt him out into the open and I've got it. I've talked to the operators of the Community Improvement Fund. They've been raising money for a new park and statue to be dedicated to the founding fathers. I've convinced them to announce inflated figures for their current fund raising campaign. Those stories are in today's papers. As part of the story, they will say that the funds are being held in the *Pioneer Insurance Company*'s safe to be taken by armored car, in two days, to the reserve bank. I figure the cash held by the fund will be too tempting for our Mr. Moon Man to pass up. He won't want to tackle an armored car or a bank; so I am betting he'll try for the Pioneer Insurance safe. And when he does we'll finally have him, by damn!"

Chief Thatcher and Steve were both silent while they absorbed this. Finally the Chief spoke, "Pioneer Insurance is in the Marmont building isn't it?"

"Right, their office is on the sixth floor. It will be easy to set a trap there. I've been over the building and have it all planned out."

Steve chimed in. "Even if the money amounts are inflated, isn't it dangerous to use the cash as bait? The Moon Man has sprung these kinds of traps before and made off with the money to boot."

Gil smiled. "But this time there won't be any money. The funds raised are safely stashed away at the First City Bank. When the Moon Man shows up this time, all he'll find are armed detectives." The head of the detective bureau smacked one fist into the palm of the other. "By damn! This time we'll nab him for sure!"

Trying to look more cheerful than he felt, Steve stood. "I'm with you Gil. Tell me what you need."

"That's the spirit Steve. The way I see it, the Moon Man has to make a try either tonight or tomorrow night. We're going to be there in force both nights. We'll have all the building entrances watched. We let the

Moon Man enter the Marmont, then we close off the exits and just like that, we have him trapped inside. I'll have a squad of detectives with me surrounding Pioneer's sixth floor office. When he breaks in, we grab him. If he avoids us and makes a run for it, the men we have at the doors will get him. Also I'll have extra patrols cruising the neighborhood. Of course, I'll want you with me Steve."

"Steve and his father were silent for a moment, then the Chief spoke. "That's a pretty big call on our manpower Gil. We can't sustain such an allocation of manpower for very long."

"It's only for two nights Chief. He thinks the money will be gone after that."

"Alright. What do you think, Steve?"

Keeping a thoughtful look on his face Steve said, "I'd like to take a look at the Marmont building. How about we go take a look at your trap Gil?"

"Good idea, Steve. We'll take my car."

From the basement garage of headquarters, it was only a short trip across downtown to the Marmont building. It was a twelve story office structure facing a major downtown avenure. They drove around the block. Steve noted there was an alley behind the building. The two side streets were filled with parked cars but would probably be deserted at night. Parking, the two detectives entered the Marmont. Past the revolving main door and crossing to the elevators Steve asked, "Other entrances?"

Gil promptly answered, "Just this and the alley. We'll have men covering both. With extra men nearby to reinforce the doors once we've got that fish-bowl-wearing menace trapped inside."

Steve nodded, "What about the roof?"

"There are no buildings close enough where he can come over the roof tops but we'll station a man there just in case he decides to rent an autogyro or something crazy. Hah!"

In the elevator Steve noted that it was one of the brand new self-operating types. Gil mumbled under his breath as he tried to figure out the controls. Steve leaned in and took a good look at the controls. The knowledge might come in handy for his fast forming plan. He found the button for the sixth floor and pressed it. Getting off there, they made a quick tour of the floor layout. Gil pointed out the three offices where he planned to station his forces. They were equally spread around those of the *Pioneer Insurance Company*. It was a large office with a wide reception area and several private offices. In one of these was an imposing floor safe. Steve would have been impressed by the massive safe but he hardly

"I'd like to take a look at the Marmont building."

glanced at it since it wasn't part of his plan. After a thorough examination of the entire sixth floor, Gil and Steve took the stairs all the way to the basement. Gil commented that the Moon Man would likely use the stairs or rear freight elevator once he got into the building. Finally they went past the closed loading dock and out the rear service door into the alley. Looking around, Gil announced, "I would imagine he'll try to make his entrance here. There is this door plus the loading door over there or he might try to climb to an upper floor window."

Steve scratched his head. "What about the fire escapes on the side streets?"

"I'll have concealed officers watching them."

"You know Gil, if I were the Moon Man, I'd conceal myself inside the building somewhere during office hours until I was ready to make my move."

"That's okay too. As long he's inside and we close off the outside doors we got him trapped."

Steve hesitated wanting to get his words just right. "Well it seems to me that this alley is the critical place. If he is going to make an entrance from the outside it will be somewhere here." Gil nodded in agreement. "Then that's where I want to be. I can probably get permission to hide inside the door of that building across the alley. I'll be totally out of sight and when he enters I can close in behind him."

Gil thought about this a moment while Steve secretly held his breath. "Steve, you're my best man. I think you're right; that would be the best place for you. I'll leave it to you to get permission from the building supervisor over there."

"Thanks Gil, I won't let you down." Steve flinched inwardly at his words. It was times like these that he most felt the tension of the narrow tight rope he walked.

After seeing Gil on his way back to headquarters, Steve went around the corner to the front entrance of the Knoph building just across the alley from the Marmont. After showing his badge, he had no trouble convincing the building manager to give him a spare key for the alley door. He was very interested in what was going on but accepted Steve's word that it was "part of an ongoing police operation." After that Steve took some time to look over the Marmont building. He strolled liesurely through the halls memorizing the layout of various floors. Lastly he examined the alley carefully. He rearranged some trash cans in the alley, before heading over to the McEwen residence.

Sue was waiting for him and they drove to a quiet Italian restaurant for lunch. While eating, Steve outlined her father's plan to catch the Moon Man. He also told her of his counter plans. After she had heard it all, she reached across the table and taking his hand gripped it with all her strength. "But why do you have to do anything, Steve? You know what Dad has planned. Why not just ignore his trap? It's far too dangerous to try and spring it. Please don't do anything so desperately foolish, dear."

Steve sighed. "Don't you see Sue? I have to. Gil has gone to a lot of trouble to make this a public challenge of the sort the Moon Man can't refuse. If he doesn't show up at the Marmont, Gil will wonder why. He may begin to believe that there is some kind of leak at police headquarters. If that happens, he may become suspicious of everyone there. I can't risk him suspecting me. The Moon Man has to appear to be after the Park Fund. Don't worry; I know Gil's plan and that will give me the advantage. I'll be fine."

Sue looked at him sadly. "Sometimes I feel we'll never be able to have a normal life. Someday I'd like to quit being your fiancé and start being your wife."

"I know Sue but now is not the time. My work is too important. There are so many people out there in desperate need of our help. People are out of work and starving, and the system is just not helping them. Take this Park Fund that Gil is using as bait. They are a legitimate organization and raising money for a park and statue is a good cause, in normal times. But to waste that kind effort on a park now when thousands of people have crucial needs is a criminal waste. But it won't be like this always. Someday there won't be a need for the Moon Man."

The rest of lunch was overshadowed by gloom. Steve took Sue directly home afterwards. Next he steered his roadster for a poorer section of town. Passing a coffee shop he pulled over and went in. Wedging himself into a narrow phone booth he closed the door and dialed a number from memory. The other end was picked up after two rings, "Hello?"

"Angel, it's me. I need to talk to you right away. We have plans to make."

"Right Boss, the usual corner in ten minutes?"

"I'll be there." Steve left the phone booth. Glancing at his watch, he started his car. He drove slowly through several neighborhoods before pulling over to idle at a curb. When the time was right, he pulled out and drove several blocks to a run-down street. He spotted the stocky figure of Angel Dargan waiting in a shadowy doorway and he waved. Angel hurried over to the roadster and slid into the passenger seat and they drove away.

"Good to see you, Boss, what's up?"

"A couple of things. First, are you getting our funds distributed?"

Angel nodded. "Several charities and an orphanage, and now I'm getting funds out to a lot of needy families."

"Good. Hopefully, there will be more soon. But first we're going to have to deal with another one of Lt. McEwen's endless plans."

"It's okay Boss, we've sprung his traps before."

"Yes, but this time we're going to use his trap as cover to work one of our own operations." He went on to outline McEwen's plans at the Marmont. He then continued, "I've deliberately left the Baker mob alone for a couple of days. Hopefully they'll drop their guard a little. I've scouted their pick up routes. Tomorrow night, when I'm supposed to be on watch at the back of the Marmont, I'll sneak away and you'll pick me up and we'll knock off Baker's courier. Then I'll drop you off with the loot and duck back to the Marmont. I'll go in the back and make some racket, let someone see the Moon Man and then duck out the back again. If I play my cards right, Gil and his men will chase themselves around the building and assume the Moon Man outsmarted them once again. Meanwhile Steve Thatcher will be at his post in the alley the whole time. It will help insure that I'm not suspected and if word gets around about the Baker courier being robbed I'm covered again because Steve Thatcher has the perfect alibi."

Angel smiled. "Good plan Boss, but how are we going to take the courier with the extra guards you say they're now using?" Steve told him and Angel nodded and then asked a couple of questions. They quickly settled on times and locations and before long Steve dropped Angel on a deserted corner near his rooming house and headed back to the station.

The rest of the afternoon passed quickly as preparations for the large stakeout went on. By six o'clock a large force of uniformed officers and detectives were on their way to the Marmont building. Things went smoothly as everyone took up their stations. Steve looked over the alley and then tried his key in the back door of the Knoph building. It worked fine and Steve took a few minutes to again check out the layout of the building. He reached the lobby and looked across it to the front door. The receptionist had left for the day but there was now a man in a security guard's uniform at the desk. He was busy reading a newspaper and did not notice Steve before he ducked back out of sight. The rest of the evening passed slowly. Steve was glad he could shelter inside the back of the Knoph building since it became colder as the night wore on.

Finally, the stakeout broke up before dawn. The officers headed home to get a few hours' sleep as they were scheduled to meet back at headquarters at noon. Steve picked up a newspaper on his way home. Sure enough, there was another story about how large the Park Fund was and how it was scheduled to go to the reserve bank tomorrow. Steve smiled to himself as he read it. Tomorrow's headlines should be even more interesting.

There was a certain tension around headquarters the next afternoon. Most officers felt that this would be the evening for action, but only Steve had any idea of just how that action would go. During McEwen's final briefing Steve took careful note of where each of the officers would be stationed; he felt confident that his plan would work perfectly. He was especially hopeful that there would be little to no gunplay. Steve did not want anyone hurt. The stakeout was to begin at seven o'clock when the building would be officially closed; although there were already plain clothes officers now prowling the halls looking for suspicious activity. McEwen dismissed everyone with orders to be ready at six p.m. Steve told Gil that he was going to slip next door to the diner to pick up a sandwich for the stakeout. While at the diner, he made a quick phone call to Angel to check on final arrangements. He was back at the station by six. The officers assigned to the Marmont checked their equipment and assembled in the police garage. There were more than a dozen plain clothes men and uniformed officers. They piled into several cars for the trip to the Marmont. Steve rode with McEwen.

As they neared the office building the quietly excited McEwen spoke, "By Damn, Steve. I really think we are going to get him tonight. He'll probably attempt to make entry in the alley so I believe you have the key spot. Once he's inside, you slam the door and keep him from escaping out the back. Don't try to take him by yourself. We'll get him inside."

"You can depend on me, Gil. I'll do everything I can."

McEwen slowed the unmarked cruiser on the side street alongside the Marmont building. Steve climbed out of the car and waved to Gil as he entered the alley. Gil waved back and drove away. Steve flicked on his pocket flash and looked over the alley carefully. The trash cans he had moved earlier were still in place. Going to a door in the rear of the Knoph building he used the key given to him by the manager. He entered a narrow hallway leading into a small vestibule with several doors off it. Steve explored the ground floor of the office building thoroughly. He found the corridor leading to the lobby facing the street one block behind the Marmont. Satisfied, he returned to the rear door. He waited just inside it, occasionally checking the alley. All remained quiet.

Time passed slowly with Steve checking the time on his wristwatch. Finally the watch indicated it was approaching ten o'clock. Steve left his post and made his way through the building. He entered the lobby through a door near the stairwell and made directly for the front door. As he crossed the lobby he saw the security guard reading a newspaper behind the receptionist's desk. His footsteps on the hard marble flooring caught the attention of the newspaper reader and he lowered the sports section he was reading to look up in surprise at Steve. He was an elderly man wearing the uniform of a night watchman. He appeared startled as he set down his newspaper and stood up. Steve was prepared for this. He swerved toward the guard and flashed his badge. "Detective Thatcher, police."

The night watchman smiled as he saw the identification. "Oh, Mr. Dunsmore mentioned that you might be around tonight. He said to give you any help I could."

Steve waved a hand. "Don't need anything right now. I'll be staking out the alley later. I'm stepping out for a bit and will be back later. I may come through here and may go through the alley, but I would consider it a favor if you did not mention to anyone that you saw me."

"Sure officer, mum's the word."

Steve thanked the guard and headed for the front door. As he stepped through he looked over his shoulder to see the night watchman settling back behind his newspaper. Once on the street he looked left and right. A car's headlights were approaching from the left. Steve stepped to the curb as the sleek roadster slid to the curb. He got in and Angel powered away. Steve said, "Right on time Angel."

Angel smiled from behind the wheel as he guided the powerful machine through the night streets. As they drove away from the business section, Steve opened up a small overnight case and took out his black robe. He threw it over his shoulders and pulled it down around him. He then removed the two pieces of the one-of-a-kind silvery globe made of special one-way Argus glass. Hooking the two halves together, he placed the globe carefully over his head. The Moon Man then pulled on a pair of thin black gloves to complete his transformation. Lastly he slipped a large automatic pistol into his robe. Ducking low to avoid any observance of his bizarre form by late night strollers, the Moon Man ordered Angel, "Circle the block once to check for anything unusual and then pull up to the alley."

"Got it, Boss."

They had left the downtown and entered another rundown block. Driving slowly, Angel pointed at a dark alley as they passed it. They turned right at the corner and cruised down an older business street. There was a surprising amount of foot traffic here. There were two bars across from a rundown hotel. All seemed to be busy; especially the hotel which had a steady stream of men entering. They turned right at the next corner to circle the block. With that many bystanders in front of the hotel, the Moon Man was hope to avoid any possible gun fight. But with gangsters, you never knew what they might do. After they had circled the block a second time, they stopped at the mouth of the darkened alley. Angel reversed the roadster twenty feet into the alley and turned off the engine and lights. The Moon Man got out of the car but leaned back in. "If everyone's on schedule, I shouldn't be long. Don't start the engine until I get back."

"Be careful Boss."

The Moon Man didn't answer. Instead he turned and was swallowed up by the darkness. Angel turned to watch but saw nothing in the alley behind the car. Then came a sudden glare of light as a door was opened in the back of the hotel and he saw the unmistakable figure of the Moon Man glide into the building and then blackness returned as the door was closed behind him.

Upon entering the hotel, the Moon Man found himself in a dim hallway. It was illuminated only by a naked bulb in a fixture overhead. He moved silently forward and reaching up unscrewed the bulb enough so that it flickered off, leaving the rear hallway in near darkness. He then moved past several closed doors, turned a corner to the right and came to another corner to the left. Peering around it he could see a short hallway that led to what must be the front door of the hotel. Across from him, a set of stairs led upward. As he watched, footsteps could be heard coming down the stairs. Ducking back the Moon Man watched a man descend as he was putting on his jacket. The fellow reached the door just in time to hold it open for someone about to enter. The Moon Man recognized the new man; he was thin, wore a suit and carried a large briefcase: Baker's courier. After letting the courier pass, the patron left the hotel closing the door behind him. The courier proceeded directly up the stairs. Drawing back into the shadows, the Moon Man waited patiently. Several patrons came and went as he waited. Soon the now familiar figure of Baker's courier came briskly down the steps. Before he could reach the front door, the silver-globed figure charged forward. Poking his automatic firmly into the courier's back, he grabbed him by the shoulder with his free hand and quietly spoke. "No sudden moves. Just step slowly backward."

The courier did as he was told and stepped backward into the hallway guided by the black robed figure. Just as the two were about to negotiate the turn into the corridor that would put them out of sight, the front door opened. A heavy set man dressed in workman's rough clothing and whistling a merry tune stepped into the small lobby. He stopped dead in his tracks as did the Moon Man and his captive. The workman's jaw dropped for just a moment and then he yelled out, "The Moon Man!" The Moon Man reached around his captive and grabbed the briefcase; with his other hand he rapped his automatic against the captive's head just hard enough to knock him to his knees. The Moon Man turned and ran for the back door as the startled patron continued to yell behind him.

Slamming through the rear door into the dark alley, he turned right and made for the roadster. Opening the passenger door he tossed the briefcase in and quickly followed it as Angel pressed the starter to bring the powerful engine rumbling to life. As he put the roadster in gear, there was a screech of brakes from another car just as it was passing the mouth of the alley. It slammed on its brakes for no apparent reason. Immediately a taxi following close behind it plowed into the rear of the braking auto with a bang. For a brief instant there was only silence, then the drivers of both cars got out and began to argue. Angel threw a shocked look at the Moon Man, "Boss, what do we. . ."

"Back up, quickly, now!"

Throwing the roadster into reverse, Angel looked over his shoulder and began driving backwards down the alley. As they passed the rear door of the hotel they nearly hit a man coming out of the rear door. He had a gun in his hand but didn't get to use it as he was forced to throw himself back into the building to avoid being hit by the speeding roadster. The alley was certainly big enough for an auto to negotiate but it was also an obstacle course of garbage cans and assorted debris. Angel dodged some but then he struck a garbage can that caromed off the bumper, ricocheted off a wall and hit another garbage can with a loud clang. Both cans ended up rolling on their sides in front of the reversing roadster. By the time the auto reached the side street it was pushing a moving pile of trash cans, boxes and assorted trash. This debris spilled out into the street with a tremendous clatter a second before the roadster followed it in a screech of brakes.

Angel looked grim as he shoved the gear shift into forward and accelerated away. The Moon Man, watching over his shoulder, saw headlights swing around the corner seconds later. Quietly he urged, "Turn right at the next corner, Angel."

The headlights turned the corner after them. "Looks like Baker's hoods. Faster." Angel opened up the powerful roadster and it surged forward. For a few moments the pursuing headlights seemed to recede and then they brightened again. Undoubtedly the pursuing car had a powerful engine as well. Desperately Angel attempted to throw off their pursuers by rounding a corner sharply but was forced to brake hard as they came up behind a city bus making a late night run. With a blast on the roadster's horn Angel swerved around it. He had been slowed however and soon the lights of the pursuing sedan had closed the distance behind them. As the Moon man watched, flashes of light came from the sedan. There was a crash that both men felt as the car was hit. Glancing nervously in the mirror, Angel questioned, "Boss?"

"Keep it steady, Angel," was the Moon Man's calm reply. He aimed his pistol back over the closed rumble seat and triggered off two quick rounds. More flashes came from the pursuing car. The Moon Man fired again. More gun flashes came from their pursuers and this time several impacts were felt as the roadster took even more damage. Steadying his pistol with both hands, the Moon Man suddenly yelled out, "Angel brake hard, now!" Rubber smoked as Angel tromped on the brakes and the big sedans' lights grew rapidly larger. Firing directly into the glare, the Moon Man emptied his automatic's magazine into the fast-approaching car. The big Packard took multiple hits. A headlight was shattered, other bullets penetrated the windshield. The sedan swerved to its right onto the sidewalk, hit a bus bench and plowed into a building's cement stoop. The Moon Man turned back in his seat as he reloaded his pistol. "Slow down. I think we've lost them."

Angel immediately eased up on the gas. "Good shooting Boss. That oughta hold'em for a while."

"I hope so. Let's head for home."

Angel guided the roadster through the night city to a row of tenement houses as the Moon Man pulled off his Argus glass helmet. He kept on the robe as they pulled over to the sidewalk. Angel set the brake and got out of his door. Steve handed him the briefcase as he slid over behind the wheel. "You know what to do with the money. Stay safe and I'll call you in a day or two."

"I better come and get the car tomorrow. We need to check over the damage. Sounded like she took a beating"

Steve nodded as he held out his gloved hand. Angel shook it and smiled at the man whom he thought was the best man alive. Then clutching the

Angel shook hands and smiled.

briefcase he disappeared into the run-down tenement.

Steve drove off slowly. He made his way toward the business section of town being careful not to attract attention. He knew there were several bullet holes in the body of the roadster, not to mention that the Moon Man's helmet was sitting on the seat beside him. He couldn't afford to be stopped by a prowling squad car. He made his way towards the Marmont building but turned down a side street two blocks away. He pulled over and stopped. Just ahead and to the right was an alley. If he took that alley he would arrive on the side street facing the side of the Marmont. When he crossed that street to the Marmont, he would certainly be seen by the detective posted to watch it. He would spread the word to other cops; they would assume that Steve Thatcher would allow the Moon Man to enter by the alley door and close it off behind him. Then the fun would start as the famous vigilante would lead them on a short but merry chase through the building before making his pre-planned escape.

He placed the silver globe over his head and got out of the car. He had taken several steps toward the alley when he heard the sound of a powerful engine behind him. Ducking behind a mailbox, he looked back. A black sedan creeping along at barely walking pace came into sight at the intersection. A small plume of steam escaping from under its hood plus one headlight out left no doubt about identity of the car. Baker's hoods must have gotten the car running, but how had they followed him? The Moon Man watched as a hood, pistol in hand, stepped out of the car and peered down at his feet. It was then that the Moon Man saw what the man was looking at in the street. A liquid trail that in the bright moonlight seemed to be made of quicksilver led around the corner and directly toward the parked roadster. It was a bright silvery trail of liquid that could only be gasoline. One of the crook's shots must have punctured Steve's gas tank. The trail of gasoline would have been easy to track in the light of the full moon. Looking back toward the roadster even now he could see liquid running along the gutter from underneath it.

As he cursed silently under his breath, the Moon Man's mind was racing. There might be a way to turn the tables on Baker's gunmen. He stood up and ran to the alley. There was a shout behind him and a revving engine. Reaching the corner he looked back. The crippled sedan screeched to a stop and armed men piled out of it. The Moon Man threw a quick shot at the hoods to slow them up and then he turned and raced into the alley. Staying low and dodging trash cans, he reached the other end of the alley as he heard his pursuers following behind him. He slowed to a quick walk and crossed the side street to the alley directly behind the Marmont. By the time he reached its back door, he had his skeleton keys out and unlocked the door. As he slipped inside, he could hear running steps and curses in the alley hard on his heels.

Having explored the building he knew just where to go. He turned to his left down a dimly lit corridor. Reaching the freight elevator, he grabbed the strap hanging from the overhead door and pulled hard. The top door lowered as the lower half rose. He could already hear voices as he grabbed the operating handle and wrenched it back. The elevator moved rapidly upward. He stopped it on the second floor. Pushing the doors open, he trotted for the main elevator. He was counting on it taking the pursuing hoods a few minutes to locate the elevator and stairwell. Pressing the first floor button in the automatic elevator, he decended to the first floor. As the door opened, he could see the night watchman look up from his newspaper. Seeing the bizarre black robed figure so startled the poor guard that he dropped his newspaper and almost fell out of his chair. The Moon Man waved his pistol menacingly and pushed the sixth floor button. As the doors closed he could see the guard grabbing for a telephone. *That should help get things moving*, the Moon Man thought grimly.

The doors opened on the sixth floor. Looking right and left he could see nothing but empty corridor. He knew full well that several detectives waited alertly within nearby offices. He pressed the Close button and fired a shot up into the roof of the elevator. The shot was oppressively loud inside the elevator itself but was probably heard as a muffled, distant pop to anyone within hearing distance. Then he slapped the Open button. When the doors slid apart, he raced out into the corridor. Within seconds a man in a suit came around a distant corner and looked toward him. He carried a gun and the Moon Man recognized him as a plain clothes detective. The Moon Man stepped quickly into the elevator and sent it downward by pressing the fifth floor button. Getting off there, he sent the elevator up to the top floor by pressing twelve. Then quickly locating the stairwell, he quietly entered it and listened. He could hear the labored breath and heavy footsteps of several men climbing the stairs. Smiling under his silver globe, the Moon Man pointed his pistol down the open center of the stairwell and triggered off two quick shots. There were shouts of surprise as his bullets ricocheted off steel and concrete as he ducked back into the fifth floor. He held the fire door slightly open and listened as an answering flurry of shots came up the stairwell. Then seconds later the door of the floor above opened and there was a shout of, "Police, throw down your weapons!"

More shots came from up the stairwell. His work done there, the Moon Man glided back to the elevator and pressed the call button. He glanced up. The dial showed the elevator passing through eight, seven, and then it stopped momentarily on six. Knowing what to expect as the dial continued downward, he flattened himself against the wall. The doors opened and nothing happened for a moment, then there was a muttered curse and Gil McEwen leaned out to look both ways. The Moon Man reached forward, grabbed the lapel of McEwen's jacket and gave the off-balance detective a hard jerk. Arms wind-milling forward, McEwen took two staggering steps out into the corridor, tripped and went sprawling on his face, his revolver clattering out of his hand. Rounding into the elevator, the Moon Man grabbed the gun hand of the detective standing there to keep himself out of the line of fire while with his other hand he grabbed the man's shirt. Pivoting, he threw the detective out of the elevator to land squarely on top of Gil McEwen; now on his hands and knees trying to retrieve his revolver off the floor. As the doors closed, the Moon Man got a satisfied look of the two policemen trying to untangle themselves. As the elevator continued downward, the Moon Man stretched upward and threw open the trap door leading to the roof of the car. Jumping up, he grabbed the edge of the trap and pulled himself upward, squeezing through the small aperture. Swinging himself onto the roof of the car, he flipped the roof door shut just before the doors below opened.

The Moon Man took stock. Things had gotten way more complicated than he had planned. He had certainly made his presence known to the police but he had not counted on Baker's hoods being there as well. It was going to be much harder carrying out his escape plan. Time was against him. He could hear loud voices below him as several men entered the elevator. He decided that the car was probably on the ground floor which made the doors opposite him the exit to the second floor. As the car began to move upward he spied a ladder built into the wall of the elevator shaft. Making a hasty decision, he jumped and grabbed the rungs of the steel ladder welded to the wall and flattened himself as the elevator car brushed past him scraping his robe. The car moved upward past him and so did his robe. It rose past his waist and he realized it was snagged on the car. He grabbed at the robe with one hand while the other clutched the ladder and pulled downward as hard as he could and still maintain his precarious balance. There came a loud ripping sound and his robe came loose in his hand. Steve breathed a sigh of relief as the car moved away from him.

Shifting his hand holds and weight he swung over to the front of the shaft. He got one foot on the door ledge and tried to get his fingers in the crack of the doors. He heard the elevator stop above him. Risking a quick glance, he could see it was thirty or forty feet above him. He couldn't get enough leverage to open the doors from that angle so he took a chance and made the small jump onto the door ledge. He didn't have very much room to stand, his Argus globe making it nearly impossible to balance himself on the narrow ledge. Still, he could get both hands on the doors to lever them apart. The elevator motor started and the Moon Man realized it was coming back down. He had only seconds before it smashed into him. He tugged harder on the doors. The elevator car got closer, less than twenty feet away. Suddenly he spied a handle; a complicated set of levers on the far side of the door. Leaning far across he tugged the handle. Pulling it down moved all the connected levers at once and the doors slid open. He dove through it just as the car passed the floor moving downward. Lying on the floor he saw the elevator doors close again.

Standing up, he looked around. He was in an empty corridor. Moving to the nearest door he read the number: 306. It was not the second floor but it would do. Running down the corridor, he rounded several corners until he reached 328. Reaching into his robe he grabbed his skeleton keys. He had worried for a second that they might have been lost when the robe was nearly torn off but they were just where he expected. The door yielded on the third key he tried. Entering, he closed the door behind him and moved through into the inner office. He crossed to the window and lifting the sash he chanced a look out to the alley below. Everything seemed quiet. Why shouldn't it be? Supposedly it was being guarded by the trusty Detective Thatcher. The Moon Man noted that the open trash can was still directly below, farther below than he had planned but there was no help for that. Turning, he quickly divested himself of his globe, robe and gloves. Taking a bundle of light cord from one pocket, he untangled it and laid it on the nearby desk. He carefully placed his gloves and automatic inside the Argus globe and then wrapped the helmet in his robe. He then tied the bundle with one end of the cord. Carrying the bundle to the window, he carefully lowered it out the window paying out the cord slowly. It was swinging slightly but he guided it over the open trash can and waited until the swinging stopped. He let out the remaining slack and the bundle entered the can but the wrapped helmet did not touch the bottom. He had planned to do this from the second floor and the cord wasn't quite long enough. Hesitating, he finally leaned out as far as he could and let the black bundle drop the short distance into the trash can. He estimated it had dropped only a foot but he still prayed silently that the irreplaceable Argus globe was not cracked or broken.

Steve moved quietly back through the office and entered the hall. He locked the office door behind him. He then dashed to the stairwell. He opened the door and listened for a moment. He heard steps and then a door slam above him. Quickly entering the stairwell, he fled down the steps. He paused one floor down as he was sure he had heard gunfire coming from somewhere in the building. Shaking his head, he continued down. At the basement door he listened but he heard nothing. He left the stairs and moved through the hallway toward the back door. He opened it and looked around. All was quiet. He was wondering what to do next when he heard footsteps. He stepped back into the building in time to see a man staggering down the corridor toward him. He was clutching his right arm in his left hand and seemed to be bleeding. Not recognizing him, Steve drew his service revolver and barked, "Police! Don't move. Raise your arms!" The man groaned and raising his arms as high as he could he leaned against the wall. Then he slowly slid down the wall with a groan. Steve went to him cautiously but he could see the gangster was in no shape to resist him. Holstering his gun, he attempted to stop the blood flowing from the man's arm. He had just managed a rough bandage when a detective, followed by a uniformed officer, came charging down the hall. They waved their flashlight beams over Steve and his prisoner, "Steve, I see you caught one."

"Sure, better get an ambulance for this one though, he's taken a slug."

"Right," the uniformed officer ran off toward the front of the building.

Things got a little bit confused after that. Officers flooded in from everywhere. Reporters began arriving even before the ambulances. As it turned out, despite all the shooting between Baker's four men and the police, no one had been killed. All four gunmen had surrendered, two of them injured. Three officers had been wounded, only one seriously. The building seemed to have taken the most damage. Before he left, Steve saw the very angry building manager giving Gil McEwen an earful of complaints and threatening to sue the city. Steve finally managed some time with McEwen when things quieted down.

"I don't know how that masked menace got away this time, Steve. Are you sure he didn't get past you?

"No Gil, the Moon Man went in the back door and then to my surprise those gunmen came running after him. But none of them got past me out the back. I can swear to that. The only one who tried was that wounded mug that I nabbed."

Gil nodded. "That was good work capturing him. By damn, I should have had you upstairs with me. Maybe then the Moon Man wouldn't have gotten away."

"What did happen up there Gil?"

Gil hesitated before speaking. "Well, it was kind of confused. We heard what sounded like gunfire and then we saw the Moon Man on the elevator. We went after him but he seemed to vanish into thin air. Then there were all these gunsels everywhere. I got another chance at him." Gil reached out and grabbed a handful of air. "He was that close to me but he got the drop on me and Hughes and vanished again into the elevator. The guy is quicker than a cat, I'll give him that."

Steve nodded sympathetically. As the police gradually packed up their operations and left, Steve turned down several offers of rides. Finally he left the building and walked down the block. He then doubled back and made his way into the alley. Using his pocket flashlight, he located the open trash can and fished out the black bundle. Carefully unwrapping it, he examined the Argus globe by flashlight. He sighed with relief when he could find no cracks or scratches on it. The robe smelled terrible after its time in the garbage can. It was also ripped and would have to be replaced. With his noxious bundle under his arm, Steve strolled along until he found a telephone booth. His first call was to Angel to tell him about the damage to the roadster and see about getting it repaired as quickly as possible. His second call was for a taxi to take him home. It had been a long day.

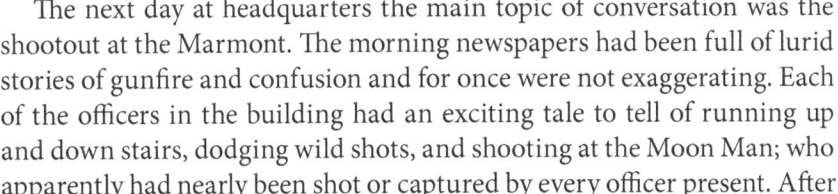

The next day at headquarters the main topic of conversation was the shootout at the Marmont. The morning newspapers had been full of lurid stories of gunfire and confusion and for once were not exaggerating. Each of the officers in the building had an exciting tale to tell of running up and down stairs, dodging wild shots, and shooting at the Moon Man; who apparently had nearly been shot or captured by every officer present. After listening to the third nearly identical story, Steve decided that it was a miracle that more officers hadn't shot each other.

Of course, Lt. Gil McEwn was furious. In Chief Thatcher's office he was completing his version of the story as Steve entered the office. "By damn Chief, we were that close! We'd have had him if he hadn't brought a bunch of hoods with him."

This remark surprised Steve. "Hold it, Gil. You don't think those gunsels were working for the Moon Man, do you?"

"Of course they were. Why else would they be with him?"

"But Gil, all of those hoods are known to be working for the Baker mob. I heard three of them confess that they were chasing the Moon Man; not working with him."

Gil snorted. "That just proves that the Moon Man is working with Baker now. That makes him more dangerous than ever."

Realizing that he would never win this argument with McEwen, Steve just shook his head. "Well, it was a good try, Gil. You nearly had him."

"Not good enough. That skunk has more luck than a leprechaun. But I'll get him, by damn!" He turned and pointed a blunt finger at Steve. "And this just goes to prove that your idea of the Moon Man taking a vacation was silly. I told you he was here all along, and up to his fish bowl in making trouble."

Steve stood up and walked to the door. As he opened it, he looked back and smiled. "Well, the Moon Man may not have been on vacation, but I could sure use one. Maybe I'll take Sue to the beach for a few days. Don't catch him before I get back, will you Gil." Steve left the office whistling.

THE END

WRITING BY MOONLIGHT

Possibly the pulp hero with the most bizarre name and appearance was the Moon Man. When it came to disguises, a cape or mask just wasn't going to cut it. The Moon Man wasn't content with anything less than a full length black robe and complete globe to cover his head, specially made of one way Argus glass that allowed one to see out of it but gave the appearance of a silvery globe from the outside. When it came to disguises he was definitely out at the far end of the spectrum.

The Moon Man was also different in his motivations. He wasn't out to bring criminals to justice; he was after their loot, which he happily stole from them at every opportunity. The Moon Man's goal was to use this money stolen from criminals and redistribute it to the poor and unfortunate suffering from the economic depression. Interestingly, he didn't restrict his thefts to the criminal element alone. He would just as soon rob the rich. Powerful men who benefitted from financial manipulations, like bankers and industrialists, were his targets. Even charities and fund raising groups who wasted their time on so-called worthy causes while average people went hungry. This "Robin Hood" mentality was probably controversial in its time. Geez, it would still be controversial today. Anyway, you can see the Moon Man was not your average masked avenger. He really stood out from the crowd in more ways than one.

It wasn't until I began writing for Airship27 that I ordered up reprints of all of the Moon Man adventures. I was quickly hooked. The unusual "Robin Hood" aspect of his story lines caught my interest as well as his relationships with the other main characters. Since he was one of the more colorful and well known heroes of the pulp era, I was a little surprised to find he was in the public domain and that Airship27 wanted stories about him. In fact, I felt exactly as Andrew Salmon describes his feelings in Airship 27's *The Moon Man, volume I*, "Are you kidding me? I can write all the Moon Man stories I want? Yup, Count me in!"

As far as writing about MM, it came very easily. Most of the original stories revolved less around the actual capers and more about Moon Man avoiding the dogged police pursuit. This made coming up with a story line easy. Pick out a dastardly villain to be robbed, add some fast paced action sequences sandwiched between efforts to stay out of the clutches of the police and season with some personal scenes thrown in to make him more human and you have a Moon Man adventure. This was a formula that Frederick Davis used time and again with great success. I hope I have done justice to Davis' creation and been successful in recreating the feel of the Moon Man's original adventures.

I didn't know a lot about Moon Man before I started researching him but now I have added him to the list of pulp heroes whose original adventures I enjoy reading again and again. For me he's now right up there with the Shadow and the Spider.

So enjoy more of the Moon Man's new adventures and maybe we'll see you again in volume III ?

GENE MOYERS - studied European and Medieval history at the University of Oregon. He is a former U.S. Army armor crewman. He worked in the High Tech industry for some time and ran a store front and internet hobby shop for several years.

An avid military gamer and role player his favorite game was *Daredevils* set in the 1930s. His love affair with the 1930s and pulps in particular stem from his first time reading a *Shadow* novel as a boy. Although interested in writing since a teen he did not turn to serious writing until 2000. He is the co-author of *GURPS Crusades* published by Steve Jackson Games and has written a *Ravenwood-Stepson of Mystery* adventure for the second volume of that series as well as a *Purple Scar* adventure—both for Airship 27. When not working on Airship 27 projects he is busy writing horror adventures for his swashbuckling character set in Colonial America.

Gene currently lives in Beaverton, Oregon with his wife and three lazy dogs.

MOON BOYS
By Greg Hatcher

Chief of Police Peter Thatcher glared across his desk at the two men seated before him. "It's been a year now. Where are we with this Moon Man character?"

Detective Gil McEwen shifted uncomfortably then looked squarely at his chief and told the truth. "Honestly, sir? Nowhere. That's the cold fact."

The chief raised an eyebrow. "But…"

"Oh, we've had skirmishes," McEwen hastened to add. "I think I've learned some things about the guy but they don't get us anywhere helpful, that's the problem. We've come up against him a number of times but we're no closer to an arrest than we ever were. All we have is the one fingerprint. The only break we got and it didn't get us anywhere, there's no match here, nor with the Feds; I even tried Scotland Yard. No record anyplace on the print. That was his only real slip. We've been close, but…" He took in a deep breath, and then let it out in a slow sigh. "He's always a step ahead of us."

Steve Thatcher leaned forward. He was only Gil's junior partner, but he was also the chief's son, and he wasn't going to let Gil fall on his sword without offering a defense. "Dad…sir…there's more to it than that. The Moon Man's stayed ahead of us but we've nabbed a lot of other guys along the way. There's the business with Commissioner Mead and the casino, the Rattler, the Red Six, the Gibson kidnapping… those were all big cases and we broke them."

McEwen snorted. "Kid, thanks for trying. But we were bystanders. That bastard Moon Man took those guys down. He's the one making war on the big crooks, taking out the competition. We get there just in time to clean up."

Chief Thatcher shook his head. "Gil, you're the closest thing to an expert on this guy that we have. What is he doing? What's his game?"

"Well…." McEwen considered it. "He's a thief. We consider him the chief suspect in at least nine major heists over the last year, discounting the copycats…"

"Copycats?" The chief blinked. "Plural?"

"It's really easy to hang a frame on the Moon Man, sir," Steve explained. "With that mirrored helmet he wears, we have no idea what he looks like, and that coupled with the fact that he almost always wears gloves... there have been several crooks that thought it would be easy to impersonate him and clean up. We've been hearing things about Moon Man-inspired gangs, even."

"But the man *himself*," the chief pressed. "What does he want? Why the costume?"

"All I've got are guesses," McEwen said. "The costume's outlandish, yeah...but nobody laughs at that fishbowl helmet now. It works for him. That helmet's Argus glass, no one can see anything of his face and the gloves and cape disguise his build, we're not even sure of his *race*. That crazy outfit marks him, sure, but he ducks behind a corner somewhere and takes it off, we got nothing. All he has to do is lose the helmet and the cape and he disappears in a city of over a million people. It's our biggest handicap. As for the rest..." He shrugged. "He's a thief. He wants money. Hell, everybody wants money, times are hard. But he's cleared over a hundred grand, that's plenty to retire on; so I'm thinking he's hooked on it. Likes the challenge, the excitement. That's how we'll get him, sir. He'll take bigger and bigger chances. We just have to be ready."

"There's something else," Steve put in. "Every place he's hit is crooked. I mean the ones we're sure of, the man himself, not the copycats. It's one of the ways we've found to weed out the fakes. The Moon Man steals from other crooks, never innocent citizens."

Chief Thatcher raised an eyebrow. "Really? I hadn't known that."

McEwen nodded, a little reluctantly. "It's true, sir. I can't deny he's done us some good, especially with the Red Six gang and that Rattler character. But I refuse to believe that it's anything more than thieves falling out. He's no hero."

"Of course not." The chief waved it away. "I'm thinking, though... maybe we might be able to anticipate him. If you're right, Gil, that he's escalating, then we ought to look at the big players still left in town that haven't been hit. Who's most likely to tempt the Moon Man? Could one of them even be the Moon Man himself?"

"Hmmm." Suddenly McEwen looked interested. "Now that's an angle. Steve? I know you were taking an interest in the racketeering unit's cases. Any ideas?"

Steve spread his hands. "Well, really, the one guy that we can single out is Frankie LeBaron. He's a big heavyset fellow, I don't think he's the Moon Man, but he's a target. Frankie owns the biggest casino in Great City. Got his start running speakeasies. Thought the Feds were going to get him on the Volstead Act a couple of years back but he got lucky. Repeal happened before they could get a case together. He made a big thing about going legit but I'm convinced he's dirty; I think that casino covers a lot of mob activity. LeBaron is trying to impress somebody. He wants the Chicago boys to think he's made the big time. There are rumors that he's putting together cash and crew for a big operation. I think he's auditioning for a seat at the table."

"That's raw meat for the Moon Man." Gil nodded. "The kid's right. I can't think of a better target."

Chief Thatcher was silent for a long moment. Finally he said, "What would it take to get inside LeBaron's operation… and stop the Moon Man once and for all? At the same time?"

"Undercover, you mean? It's possible," Steve said. "It would have to be a new face, someone LeBaron doesn't know."

"Someone like you, kid." McEwen clearly thought the idea had possibilities. "I think you'd make a good blackjack dealer, something like that. We can put together a good story. I got a friend at Treasury, he knows some of Hoover's boys. They'll play ball. We can swing it so it looks like Chicago recommended you."

Chief Thatcher was nodding now too. "I like it. Steve, it'll be risky, but I think the risk might be worth it."

"I can stand the risk," Steve said.

And it was true. Risk was nothing new to Steve Thatcher, because unbeknownst to the other two men in the room, he himself was the mysterious Moon Man.

That afternoon, on a sidewalk in a run-down Southtown neighborhood, Steve was getting another scolding, this time from his fiancée: Sue McEwen, Gil's daughter. They were walking arm-in-arm past a row of brownstones. Some of the neighborhood kids were playing stickball in the street.

"Why in the world would you agree to something like that?" Sue was furious and not bothering to hide it. "It's bad enough that you are on this crazy crusade to begin with, with both your father and mine sworn to arrest the Moon Man, and every crook in town gunning for him, but now you're taking on a third identity that's even *more* dangerous? Do you have a death wish?"

"Whoa, whoa, whoa, it wasn't like that," Steve said. "Dad was raking Gil over the coals about the Moon Man and I was just trying… it just kind of escalated," he finished, helplessly.

His fiancée was not placated. "It's bad enough you put on that damn fishbowl and go out at night to…"

"To *help*," Steve said, firmly. "Look at these kids. That's who it's for, Sue." He pointed at a ginger-haired boy in a leg brace, happily chasing a ball that had been hit towards him. "The O'Leary boy, there… the Moon Man's haul from the Black Hand numbers operation is paying for his treatment. We've got the street clinic operation to think of. All that cash would be sitting useless in some evidence locker if not for the Moon Man."

Sue relented. She smiled up at Steve. "I know. I even understand. But how did you let yourself get…"

"I had no choice, I told you." Steve sighed. "Gil somehow got wind of the fact that I'd been asking the vice guys about Frankie LeBaron. I couldn't pretend to be ignorant, and at least this way I'm on the inside, I'll be able to work around the police like I always have."

Sue considered this. They walked in silence for a while, then she burst out, "Steve, why are you even a cop?"

"Huh?" Steve blinked.

"I'm serious," she said. "The way you talk about the police, the unfairness of things… do you even believe in the law any more?"

Now it was Steve's turn to fall into a thoughtful silence. Finally he said, "I still believe in the law, yes. I'm not sure I believe in people as much as I used to. Crooked cops, crooked politicians…you know as well as I do how many of those I've been up against. The good guys have so many rules, and the bad guys don't have any. In a city as corrupt as this one has become, sometimes…. sometimes it takes someone who's willing to go outside the rules to get things done."

Sue shook her head. "I don't know. Who gets to decide? What if every cop had your *rules-are-optional* attitude?"

Steve stopped and took her by the shoulders. "Are you asking me to stop? To give up the Moon Man entirely? I've done some real good. You know I have."

"I know." The expression in Sue's clear blue eyes was more serious than Steve had ever seen from her before. "But I don't like what the Moon Man's turning you into, Steve. I can understand fighting criminals and corruption. I can understand trying to help the poor families hit hardest by this Depression. But it's turned into a war now. The Moon Man's at war with everyone, whether you want him to be or not. I have nightmares about you shooting it out with Dad some night. You know he'll never give up."

"Trust me, I know." Steve's voice was bleak. "I've never fired on a cop trying to do his duty, Sue, and I never will. You have to believe that. I'll let myself be taken before I do."

She nodded.

After a minute, Steve said, "You didn't answer my question."

"About quitting? I'd never ask that of you, Steve. But…" Sue let out a long sigh. "Maybe there's a better way? Something where you're not everyone's target all the time?"

"Maybe." Steve grinned, trying to banish the melancholy that threatened to overtake them both. "I'll think about it, Sue. I promise. Enough for today. Let's go see what Angel's kids can do."

"No! Damn it, Isaac! Your *left!* Keep your left arm up!" Angel Dargan's tobacco-harsh voice was like the bark of an impatient seal. "I could throw horseshoes through that opening!"

"Yessir, Mister Angel!" The fourteen-year-old boy in the ring nodded and obediently raised his left arm, just in time to deflect a hard right from his equally youthful sparring partner.

"And you, Joshua," Dargan added. "Quitcher dancin' around! Close in!"

"Uhuh." Joshua's reply was something between a pant and a grunt. The two boys circled each other warily, each looking for a possible opening. Isaac took a tentative swing. Joshua ducked it easily and launched a swing of his own. Isaac tried to duck in turn but the punch still clipped the side of his headgear and spun him. He sat down hard. A brief titter of laughter erupted from the small group of spectators, four more boys between the ages of twelve and fifteen.

"That's enough of that. We don't laugh at somebody doing his best. Next kid who does, he goes a round with *me*, and we'll see who laughs then." Angel Dargan had been a professional boxer once, and he would still have been in the ring if not for the arthritis in his arm. Like many athletes who age out of their chosen sport, he had taken up coaching as a way to keep his hand in.

Of course, the coaching was just a hobby. Dargan's true vocation was his work aiding the Moon Man. The Angel had fallen on hard times after his ailments had taken him out of the fight game, and it was Steve Thatcher that had found him in a Hooverville not far from the Great City Mission and offered him a job. At first Steve had not dared to confide his identity to Dargan, but after a few close calls where the Moon Man had only been saved by Dargan's quick wit and steady gun hand, he'd told him everything, and now Angel was a full partner in the operation. He'd even substituted as the Moon Man for Thatcher once or twice.

But his major responsibility was finding candidates for the charities the Moon Man supported with his thefts from Great City gangsters. Angel Dargan was the main conduit between the poor of Great City and the money the Moon Man found for them. He had been the one to discover the O'Leary family and bring them to the storefront clinic the Moon Man secretly financed in Southtown, along with many others.

But sometimes money wasn't enough. The boys of the Southtown neighborhoods, especially, needed some kind of direction in their lives. And Angel missed boxing. With the aid of his old friend Barney, who owned the gym, and some minor financial assistance from the Moon Man funds, Dargan had started the Southtown Youth Boxing League a month ago. The kids were coming along well, he reflected. And he was grateful Barney didn't have a *no-coloreds* rule like some of the gyms in town did.

"So is this where we find the great fighters of the future?" came Steve Thatcher's voice.

Dargan's face split in a toothy grin as he turned to see Steve and Sue enter. "Hey now! How you guys doin? Take a break, fellas," he added, addressing the boys. Josh and Isaac both obediently dropped their arms to their sides, and clambered down to the floor with an air of relief. The other four turned to stare in curiosity at Steve and Sue, who very clearly were not from Southtown.

"How is the grand experiment going?" Sue wanted to know. "Let's meet your boys."

"Sure. Come on over, fellas." Dargan beckoned the boys over to him. "These two that were sparring are Josh and Isaac." Josh was a pale, skinny youth with a head of unruly black curls, and Isaac was a dark-skinned boy with a very short buzzcut. "And these other four are T.J., Mickey, Red, and Paco. Come meet Mister Thatcher and Miss McEwen, boys, they helped put this thing together." T.J. was a gangly, dour-looking kid with straw-colored hair. Mickey was the shortest, built like a fireplug, with short black hair held in place with a little too much tonic. Red was, as one would expect, a redheaded boy with a furious splash of freckles covering his entire upper body, made more apparent by the red satin trunks he was wearing. Paco was the oldest, a Hispanic boy of fifteen with darkly suspicious eyes.

"I see our mutual friend came through with the gloves and trunks," Sue said slyly. "You look very professional, boys. Just like real boxers."

"They *are* real boxers," Dargan said. "Getting there, anyway. If Isaac can keep his left up, and Josh quits backing up all the time, and Mickey quits tryin' for the KO right away, and…"

"Aw, let 'em up, Angel," Steve said, smiling. "You're embarrassing them. Are you enjoying learning about boxing, boys?"

There was a moment's awkward silence, then Mickey burst out with, "I like knowing how to *fight*. I'm sick of being picked on."

That got Steve's attention. "Is someone picking on you?"

"Somebody's picking on the *neighborhood*." Dargan's voice was bleak with disgust. "It's Frankie LeBaron's boys. He's trying to corner the action here in Southtown. Numbers, horses, all of it. Not official, like, but we know the muscle's all Frankie and his crew at the Casino."

Steve regarded the boys for a moment. "Have any of you seen something you can tell the police?"

This only got him snorts and laughter. "Yah, sure," T.J. said. "Cause cops always help out here in Southtown. Sometimes they even show up when you call 'em."

Dargan bristled, but Steve waved it away. "It's all right, Angel. They probably have their reasons for feeling as they do. But you should know, boys, I'm a police detective myself, and I'm here listening right now. If there's anything…anything at all…you can think of that might help us get LeBaron, you can tell me and I swear to you it won't be ignored. Not all of us are on the take. I'm not."

The boys looked at Steve with embarrassment now. Except Paco, who still looked suspicious. Steve wished he knew what was bothering the fifteen-year-old, but couldn't think of a way to zero in on it without making it worse.

Finally Mickey said, "Mister, I appreciate you asking, but cops aren't going to get it done. Frankie's too big."

Steve said, "Nobody's too big. Sooner or later we'll get him." But a little voice in the back of his head whispered, *Really? That's not what you told Sue. If cops can get Frankie, why bother with your Moon Man act?*

Almost in answer, T.J. said, "The Moon Man could take LeBaron. He's taken out a lotta big crooks."

This amused Steve. "The Moon Man's just another big crook himself, isn't he?"

"He is not!" Paco had been silent up till that point, but now his face was hot with anger. "He helps people! Tell him, Mister Angel!"

"Yes," Sue said in a voice rich with suppressed laughter. "Tell us, Angel."

"C'mon now, fellas," Angel pleaded. "You shouldn't be talking about that stuff."

"No, I'm curious now," Steve said, growing serious. "Paco, do you know something about the Moon Man? Angel, what's he talking about?"

Angel spread his hands helplessly and started to speak, but Paco cut him off. "Like I'm going to spill to a cop. Look, I'm sorry, mister, if you're friends with Mister Angel you're probably okay but you're still police. The Moon Man helps neighborhood folks, that's all you need to know. You want to go after somebody, go after guys like LeBaron."

"But…" Steve's frustration was starting to show, and the hell of it was, he agreed with the kid. But Paco clearly knew more than he should about the Moon Man, about the LeBaron operation. Steve could tell from Angel's face that he didn't know what Paco was on about, either. Sue laid a hand on his arm, code for *let it go for now,* and Steve closed his mouth.

Dargan broke the tension by saying, "Okay, fellas, we're done for today. Go shower and get dressed. See you back here on Thursday and we'll try again to turn you into real boxers."

The boys obediently filed away to the locker room doors in the back. Steve waited until they were out of earshot and then hissed, "What the hell, Angel?"

Dargan shrugged. "Boss, I dunno. They ain't getting the Moon Man stuff from me, but they ain't stupid, either. We been doing this long enough that maybe some of 'em are guessing about where the neighborhood gets its improvement funds. They have parents and parents say things."

"Little pitchers, big ears," Sue agreed. "The more you pressure them, the more they'll clam up."

Steve wasn't satisfied. "This was more than that, though. Paco knows something. Something about LeBaron's operation. If I can figure what it is, maybe I can get ahead of it and there'd be no need to go undercover at the casino. That would solve both our problems," he added, with a tight smile at Sue. "Angel, do you have addresses on these kids?"

Dargan clearly didn't like the idea. "Boss, these are just kids. I don't think we need to be shaking them down for info…"

"No shakedown, I promise." Steve smiled, then grew serious. "But I think Paco and his family might be in trouble. If they are, they could use some help; either from cop Steve Thatcher or from the Moon Man."

Dargan considered it, then nodded reluctantly.

Sue sighed and said, "Well, there goes dinner."

Paco's family lived in a small apartment over the bodega they operated, not far from the gym. Steve took a position in an alley across the street, where he could watch the entrance. He wasn't sure, exactly, what he was looking for, but staking the place out seemed like his best chance. *I'll give it a couple of hours,* he decided. *At least until they close. If nothing happens, I'll go knock on the door. Maybe I can talk to Paco's parents, somehow persuade them that I'm a cop worth trusting.*

It took less than an hour for something to happen. As the sun set and Steve could see a middle-aged, thin Hispanic man…Paco's father?… begin the work of pulling the fruit carts back inside the store, two broad-shouldered figures in dark suits and fedoras approached. The storekeeper froze in fearful recognition.

"Howya doin?" The taller of the two suited men spoke with a hearty cheer that was somehow ominous. "You got the dough we asked for yesterday?"

The storekeeper's shoulders slumped. "I have some," he said slowly. "Not all. But…"

"That's too bad," the tall man said. "Really. Because now…" He reached into his jacket.

Gun in a shoulder rig, Steve realized, and started across the street, reaching for his badge. Then he stopped, shocked.

A rock flew straight and true at the gunman's head. It knocked him sideways and he whirled, stumbling, still trying to get his pistol out of the shoulder holster. His partner whipped out a snub-nosed .38 and another rock knocked it out of his hand. He swore savagely and clutched his wounded hand to him.

More rocks flew. The men in suits stumbled around in a ragged circle, trying to see where the assault was coming from. The barrage of rocks continued unabated as, to Steve's astonishment, three black-clad figures in silver helmets, brandishing baseball bats, ran towards the two gunmen. The tall gunman cursed and aimed his pistol at the middle of the three, but a rock spoiled his aim and then the silver-headed figures were on him. They rained blows on both of the gunmen and the two men in suits fell to the street. The middle one said in a low growl, "You just get out of here, and don't come back. Tell LeBaron Southtown is off limits. It's under the protection of the Moon Boys!"

The tall gunman struggled to his feet and tried to snarl a reply but a hard blow to the stomach from a baseball bat sent him to his knees. He vomited.

Steve finally recovered from his astonishment and started across the street again. "Police!"

The Moon Boys broke and ran. Steve saw that they were not wearing true Moon Man helmets, but leather football helmets over domino masks, all painted silver. The two gunmen tried to sit up. Steve skidded to a halt and flashed his badge. "Police. Just stay where you are." He knelt and picked up the pistols the two men had dropped.

"Ain't you gonna chase those kids?" the shorter of the two wailed. "They *attacked* us! Right here in the street!"

"Yes they did." Steve nodded. "Right after you threatened this man with a gun. Can't say I really blame them." The man started to protest and Steve shook his head. "Save it. I saw it all. Sir," he addressed the storekeeper, who looked as frozen with shock as Steve had been. "Can you please call the precinct so we can get these two off your doorstep and into a cell where they belong?"

The storekeeper nodded and disappeared into the bodega. Steve regarded the two men on the pavement with amusement. "So, you work for Frankie LeBaron? Is that what I heard?"

The tall man spat blood. "Shove it, shamus. I ain't saying nothing till I get a lawyer."

"Suit yourself." Steve glanced at the bodega entrance. He wondered if the storekeeper had seen what Steve had… that during the barrage of thrown rocks, the Moon Boys had not come from the alley next to the building, but from the bodega itself. They had been inside the building.

This almost certainly meant that Paco was one of them. *Figure three from the store, three more on the roofs with rocks at the ready… that's six in all,* Steve realized. *They had the place staked out same as me. They were waiting for these guys. And if Paco's one of them… that leaves five. Angel's group. Red, T.J. Mickey, Isaac, and Josh.*

There was no proof, but Steve was sure of it. *So not only is the Moon Man inspiring these kids… but thanks to Angel, he's also financing their fight training. They're my responsibility. But what should I do?*

Four hours later, at the precinct house, Steve was no closer to an answer. Gil McEwen had joined him and together they were watching as Detective Rodrigo Sanchez tried to get a statement from the storekeeper. The grocer was so terrified that most of his English had deserted him, though they had determined that his name was Rafael Garcia and he was the owner of

A hard blow to the stomach sent him to his knees.

the bodega, and he had been threatened before.

"Ask him if he knew the gunmen," Gil said. "Did they mention who they worked for? Who was running the protection racket?"

Sanchez nodded. *"¿Sabía usted que estos hombres? ¿Dijeron que los empleados?"*

The storekeeper shook his head violently and rattled off a string of Spanish so rapid that it looked as though even Sanchez was having a hard time following it. Finally Sanchez held up a hand and Garcia fell silent.

Sanchez looked up at the other two detectives. "Okay. He says he doesn't know the men, except that they are very bad men, they have beaten others in his neighborhood that could not pay the money they asked. He says he does not know who they work for. He keeps repeating that he knows nothing, he is just a shopkeeper. I can't seem to shake him of the idea that he's under arrest. He says he cannot afford to go to jail, his family needs him."

"Oh, for..." Gil looked exasperated. "Did you explain we're the good guys?"

Sanchez shrugged. "Talk's cheap. They don't trust police in Southtown. We're lucky he was willing to talk to us at all." He sighed. "Although I'm getting the impression that he's only doing that much because he thinks we'll jail him if he doesn't. He keeps coming back to the assertion that he's just a storekeeper. If Steve hadn't been there I doubt he'd have pressed charges on his own."

Garcia nodded. *"Si. Si.* I am just selling groceries."

Gil snorted and beckoned Steve to join him out in the hallway. "The two hoods are standing mum. Garcia will fold up like a cheap tent once their lawyer gets started on him, he's scared to death. And no link anywhere to LeBaron."

"The gang kids were sure." Steve rubbed his jaw. It was shaping up to be a long night.

"I bet." Gil's voice was a low growl of frustration. "Moon kids. That's all I need. You say they were all dressed like the Moon Man?"

"Not helmets," Steve said. "Improvised. Like kids dressing up as the Moon Man for Halloween. Football headgear and masks underneath. All silver." He did not add that he had a good idea who they probably were. Steve told himself that he needed real proof before making an accusation like that, but the truth was that he didn't want Paco and his friends to have to face McEwen's almost pathological hatred of the Moon Man. *It's my problem,* he thought. *I'll have to find a way to make them stop before they get into real trouble.*

Gil shook his head in disgust. "Hell of a thing, a bunch of kids making a hero out of a crook like that. What happened to kids looking up to ballplayers?"

"The Moon Man's taken down a lot of big crooks," Steve said. "And Southtown's had a lot of bent cops. I can see why these boys would look up to the kind of…"

"Are you defending them?" Gil's face screwed up into a furious scowl.

"I *understand* them," Steve said. "I understand feeling frustrated with the police, and frustrated with the fact that poor people get less justice than rich people. You and I know that there are rules we have to stick to, but these street kids don't see the rules. They just see that the police can't hurt the mob, but the Moon Man can. Tell me you don't get frustrated yourself sometimes, Gil. Look at all the time we've spent today trying to link those two hoods to LeBaron's operation. You know it, I know it, poor Rafael Garcia in there probably knows it. But we can't do a damn thing about it without actual proof."

Gil glared at Steve for a moment, then nodded. "Yeah. I guess we better get some. Speaking of, I fixed it with my buddy at Treasury. You ready to go to work for LeBaron?"

"Sure," Steve said. "Starting when?"

"Tomorrow." Gil sighed. "First thing in the morning. We're not getting anywhere with this. I think we can take the rest of the night off. You wanna grab some chow?"

"Can't. Got an errand."

This wasn't exactly a lie. Though the errand wasn't Steve Thatcher's, but rather his alter ego's. Steve thought that the Moon Man should look in on Paco and his friends. A police detective wouldn't even get a hearing, but Steve hoped they'd listen to their hero if he told them to stop.

Paco Garcia was weary but triumphant. He had doubled back to the bodega after ditching his Moon Boy disguise, just barely in time to be present when Papa went down to the precinct house with the detectives, so that he could keep the store open even with his father gone. Running the grocery all by himself all afternoon had been tiresome, but Paco was the only one who could do it. His mama was back in bed again today. Her consumption was getting worse as the summer gave way to fall. Most days she kept to her bed, a pile of blood-flecked tissues on the nightstand evidence of how difficult breathing had become.

The tuberculosis had got hold of Paco's mama late last year and now if she endured any stress at all, even just climbing the hall stairs, it often led to painful fits of coughing. The doctor at the Southtown clinic had said that Mama should relocate to a warmer, drier climate like Arizona if she was ever to get a chance to fully heal, but for the Garcias that was so impossible it might as well have been the planet Mars. The best Paco and his father could do was to try to keep her calm and quiet, and between them they had managed to keep house and run the bodega over the summer months without placing any burden on Mama. School started in a couple of weeks, though, and both his mama and papa were determined that Paco would graduate high school. That would mean that Papa would have to take care of Mama and run the grocery largely on his own.

It was all about money, Paco knew. When there was no money, there were no choices, not really. The Garcias knew that since Mr. Roosevelt had taken office a year and a half ago he had tried to change things for people who were hurt most by the Depression, they had heard him talking on the radio about a New Deal, but Papa had refused to go on the dole and instead renewed his efforts to keep the grocery open and running. "People must eat," he said. "And we sell food. We must just be careful and work harder." He had let his two employees go and Paco had stepped in. They had held their own, but that was all; Paco's father always sounded firm, but in reality he extended credit to many neighborhood families far longer than he would have if he was truly the ruthless business man he pretended to be. Still, they got by.

Then Mama had gotten sick. There were no hospitals in Great City that extended charity treatment for consumptives; mostly because there was no real treatment, other than bed rest and trying to keep the environment warm and dry. It became slowly apparent that no matter how hard Paco and his father worked, they were never going to get enough money to move somewhere Mama could get better, and as the spring turned to summer it became impossible even to afford a doctor.

But one night Mr. Angel had come. Somehow he had found out about Mama's illness and he told Papa and Mama that there was a new clinic open in Southtown, a charity clinic free to all that needed it. "We got quite a few lungers," he had said. "Your missus here, it sounds like we might be able to help. Got some good docs working there, they know about stuff like these new sulfa drugs. Helped a bunch of folks."

Papa had shaken his head, not daring to believe. "But the money..."

"You just let me worry about the money," Angel had said. "We got us a benefactor."

Papa and Mama were too grateful to question, but Paco had heard the word 'benefactor' before, and usually that meant mob money. There was still a lot of crime in Southtown, even after Repeal. Places that had begun as speakeasies had diversified their operations to numbers, horses, even dope and prostitution. Businesses that should not have prospered nevertheless were weathering hard times due to back-room operations financed by gangsters like Frankie LeBaron. It was an open secret, and everyone knew the cops were paid to look the other way.

Paco did not want his family to fall under the heel of someone like LeBaron, no matter how desperate the times had become. His papa was too trusting. Paco wanted to be sure that the clinic's offer didn't come with strings attached.

So one night Paco had followed Angel Dargan to the clinic, and he had seen Angel meeting with his 'benefactor' in the alley behind the building. A black-clad figure in a silver helmet had handed Angel a suitcase full of cash. "I see the Moon Man persuaded the Black Hand to make a donation before the cops mopped 'em up," Angel had said.

"I can be persuasive when I need to be. All it took was a gun in Bronsky's back to help him find charity and mercy for the less fortunate." The helmeted figure laughed. "He couldn't hand it over fast enough. Anyway, the O'Learys need that money for their boy's polio treatment a lot more than Bronsky needs it where he's going."

The Moon Man! Paco was amazed and delighted. Everyone in Southtown knew that the Moon Man had brought about the downfall of many big crime operations, but people just assumed he kept the profits himself. The revelation that the famous thief was actually helping the neighborhood changed Paco's attitude towards Angel Dargan instantly; dark suspicion was suddenly hero worship. When Angel had posted the flyers announcing the formation of the youth boxing league, Paco had been among the first to sign up.

He had found the other boys in the new league to be kindred spirits; all of them came from poor families, all of them were resentful of the mob presence in Southtown, and all of them were contemptuous of the police's inability to do anything meaningful about it. When Paco had confided what he had discovered about the Moon Man to them, it was Mickey who suggested the idea of forming a kind of junior auxiliary. They could make their own Moon Man outfits and join the fight themselves.

"Isn't that dangerous?" T.J. had asked. "Those guys have guns."

"We can do it." Josh had been silent at first, but his dark eyes sparkled at the idea of taking action themselves. "Those guys going around trying to get protection money, we can get the drop on them, I know it. There's only two of them, usually. They're working their way down from Seventh Avenue, they hit my folks at the bakery last night. That means it's Paco's folks and Red's on Ninth, day after tomorrow. We can be ready; there's all that football gear at the gym, left over from last winter. Barney'll never miss it. We can paint some helmets silver. Still need masks though."

"I can get those," Red volunteered. "Mom's got a bunch of old costume stuff in a box in her sewing room. Leftovers from when we helped with the school play last year."

And so it had gone. Each had contributed something to the plan and by the end of the following day the Moon Boys were ready. Today had been their first real victory, and Paco was still feeling exhilarated.

Night had fallen, and his father had returned hours ago. Supper had been subdued. Papa had assured Mama that there would be no more trouble from the bad men, and the police had promised to protect them, but he had not sounded very sure. Paco lay in his bed, staring at the ceiling, but sleep would not come. He wondered if there was something the Moon Boys could do.

There came a tap at the window. Paco could see a silver-helmeted figure squatting on the fire escape. At first he thought it was T.J., but then he looked again. It was the real Moon Man!

The window slid up. "Paco Garcia?"

Paco swallowed, hard. "Yes, sir."

"I'm the Moon Man." The helmet muffled the voice and made it sound distant, unearthly. "You and your friends stopped Frankie LeBaron's boys today."

"Yes." Paco decided there was no point in denying it.

"It was very dangerous, you took a terrible chance. Those men could have killed you."

"We were careful!" Paco said, stung. "We had four pails of rocks, we were hidden, we wore our masks! We planned very carefully!"

The Moon Man held up a hand. "You did well. You saved your papa. I respect that. Honest. But..." The helmeted figure's shoulders slumped a little. "I cannot...what I do, the choices I make, I can do these things because I am alone. The risk is all mine. When you dress like me, men will think you are with me. They could attack you, trying to get to me. I can't have that on my conscience. The work that I do, it's..." He ran out of words. Finally he said, "Look, you boys just have to stop, before you get hurt."

Paco was still bristling. "Why? Who appointed you to fight these guys? Do you think you're the only one who cares? Who makes choices? This is our home. We want to help. We have a right…"

"Dead children can't help me." The Moon Man's voice was flat and final. "And LeBaron or men like him will not hesitate. They will shoot you dead and go home and sleep well. They don't care." Seeing Paco's crestfallen expression, he relented a little. "But I can use a different kind of help from you. You knew LeBaron was sending those men, knew far enough in advance to prepare an ambush. How? Where are you getting your information?"

"We hear things," Paco shrugged. "It's our neighborhood. We live here. People talk, they think we're not paying attention. We could tell LeBaron's men were moving in a pattern." He explained how the boys had figured it out.

"That was good work," The Moon Man admitted. "I had heard rumors but I had no idea he had gotten so far." Behind the silvered glass of the helmet, Steve's expression was one of rueful disgust. *No wonder the cops can't get anywhere in Southtown. LeBaron's protection racket was common knowledge in the neighborhood and no one trusted the police enough to tell us. I've got to put a stop to this… somehow.* "LeBaron will probably send other men," he mused. "He needs cash. He's building a reserve… but why?"

"Guns," Paco said. "He is getting shipments of guns."

The helmeted figure stiffened in surprise. "What? How?"

Paco looked surprised. "His men have been talking," he explained. "We heard them, more than once. We've been trying to listen in when they come to our neighborhood." He grew animated. "Sir, we aren't just children playing. We take turns following them, we're careful. We hear many things."

"What else have you heard?" The Moon Man leaned forward. "Where are the guns coming from? Why does LeBaron want them?"

Paco thought hard. "They are coming by boat," he said after a moment. "I'm pretty sure that's what T.J. said. Sometime in the next couple of days."

"That's very helpful." The Moon Man fell silent for a moment, thinking. *By boat. Europe. German munitions, most likely.* Maybe they could get increased patrols down at the docks, cops in plainclothes. He'd have to put Gil on it; no. Too much chance of some crooked cop getting word to LeBaron. He had to get ahead of LeBaron on this somehow. *If Frankie's looking to become the arms merchant to the Chicago mob…*

"We can ask around," Paco offered. "Find out other things. Let us help. Please."

The Moon Man didn't answer right away. Finally he said, "All right. But carefully. You mustn't take chances. If you find out anything, you can tell Mr. Angel at the gym, he can get a message to me. Understand?"

"Yes! Thank you!" Paco was elated.

"I mean it," The Moon Man jabbed a gloved finger at Paco. "You must never place yourselves in danger. Ever! Just keep your ears open for anything you might hear about LeBaron."

"No danger. I promise."

"All right, then." The Moon Man inclined his head forward in acknowledgement, and then was out the window and up the fire escape. If he had realized what Paco's delighted grin meant, he might not have been so quick to depart. But it had been a while since Steve Thatcher was a teenager, and he had forgotten that a fifteen-year-old boy has a very different idea of what "no danger" means than an adult does.

The casino floor manager regarded Steve Thatcher with an expression that was not quite disapproval and not quite skepticism. "Steve? That's your name? From Chicago?"

"That's right." Steve tipped his fedora back and inserted a toothpick into the corner of his mouth. "Thought Frankie was told I was coming." He hoped his mustache wasn't crooked. He'd spent far too much time that morning trying to apply it, and he could still smell the slight tang of spirit gum. Also, the damn thing itched. But better safe than sorry.

"Mmp." The manager shrugged and held out a hand. "Well, welcome, I guess. I'm Morty. We better go upstairs and meet Frankie." He gestured at Steve to follow him. They threaded their way past the roulette wheels and card tables to a carpeted stairway in the back that led to an upper hall. Morty opened a heavy oaken door at the end of the hall and gestured Steve to step ahead of him. Steve entered the office, and Morty followed behind and stood just to Steve's left.

Frankie LeBaron was sitting behind a huge marble-top desk. Behind him was a wall hidden by maroon velvet drapes that hung from ceiling to floor. The marble was a deep blue with veins of pale blue-white running through it. Atop that was a dark green desk blotter and, at a perfect forty-five degree angle to the left of it, a gold fountain-pen set in a teakwood stand. Steve doubted the desk got much use as an actual writing desk; Frankie had people for that. There were no chairs for visitors. Only Frankie was allowed to be seated, apparently. It figured. The richly appointed desk was a status symbol. This was a throne room.

As for the man behind the royal desk, LeBaron himself also looked regal, in a decadent Roman-emperor sort of way. He was a bloated Nero in a pinstripe suit. His face was round and red, with a potato nose between two heavy-lidded eyes. His steel-gray hair was thinning but not yet gone; what was left had been combed over the top and glued into place with pomade that shone almost blue under the unflattering ceiling light. "Steve from Chicago," he said without ceremony.

"Yeah." Steve let it hang. Two could play that game.

LeBaron grunted. "I had a call yesterday from Tony Bartell, he recommended you. Tony's a pal. So I said I'd take a look, see whatcha can do. I didn't guarantee him nothing though."

Steve nodded. That phone call had cost Gil some favors at the Bureau, but it had paid off. Bartell was about to turn state's evidence on a number of Chicago mob figures in exchange for a lighter sentence, but the news hadn't gotten out yet. FBI men had been quietly arresting major Chicago crime figures for the last couple of days based on what Bartell was giving them. The phone call had been carefully supervised. Bartell was cooling his heels under guard in a downtown hotel, surrounded by G-men; there had been four men with guns at the ready if Bartell had tried to warn LeBaron of anything. But it looked like the mob stoolie had played ball.

After a moment, LeBaron shifted his bulk and looked directly at Steve. "So you're here. What happened in Chicago?"

Steve had been carefully coached on this and given suitable names to drop. "I was working for Sonny Marucci. One of his guys spilled to the Feds and they were picking everybody up. Anybody didn't get scooped up had maybe a couple of hours to get out of town. I made a couple of phone calls and they said if I came out to Great City that Frankie LeBaron might have some room for a guy who's looking to earn."

LeBaron raised an eyebrow. "You bring Federal trouble into my house?"

Steve shook his head. "Naw. I got away clean. Nobody here knows me. Anyway, their case is Marucci and his made guys. They got them. I'm just a working stiff."

LeBaron nodded, accepting it. "So what can you do?"

Steve spread his hands. "What've you got?"

"Licensed to carry?" At Steve's nod, LeBaron looked over to Morty, who stepped forward. "Morty? We got room for a security man?"

Morty nodded. "Actually, we got a couple openings," he said. "Yesterday there was…"

LeBaron waved him to silence. Steve suppressed a grin. He was sure

Morty was referring to the two men the Moon Boys had taken out at the Garcia grocery. LeBaron went on, "Okay. Well, here's the setup." He touched a hidden button somewhere under the desktop and the velvet drapes behind him parted, revealing an expansive glass window that looked out over the main floor of the casino. "We do a lot of business here, lotta money moving around. So we got strict controls. Mostly people buy chips from the dealers, so every dealer has a cashbox under the table. Every three hours we do a cash drop, we switch out the full for an empty and walk the cashboxes back to the count room. We got two guys walking the cash back, we got Morty here on the floor watching the dealers."

"Ever had a problem with dealers skimming?" Steve knew the probable answer but figured it was something a Chicago guy would ask.

LeBaron merely snorted. Morty said, "Just once. Guy was gone the same afternoon."

"Yeah? What happened?" Steve let a little smirk show. He was sure that 'gone' meant dead. Skimming was a killing offense. But it would be in character to prod a little, make one of them say it.

Morty scowled. "Gee, I dunno, maybe he went to visit his sick grandma in Schenectady. What do you think happened?"

"Just curious." Steve shrugged. "Wondered if I might be taking a guy to see his sick grandma one of these days."

At that LeBaron let out a short, humorless chuckle. "We'll see," he said. "I doubt it'll be necessary. We got a good bunch of guys now. Morty, take him along and put him on the floor. He can watch the action there until it's time to do the drop, then he can join the crew walking the boxes to the count room. He can partner with Jonesy down by the blackjack tables. Jonesy'll show him the ropes." He swiveled in his chair and gazed out over the casino floor, signaling that the royal audience had ended.

As Steve followed Morty out of the office, he thought: *That's the first hurdle, anyway. I'm in. Let's see where I can take it from here. At least this fake mustache stopped itching.*

At the same time Steve Thatcher was being interviewed by LeBaron, another meeting was taking place that would prove to have unforeseen consequences for the Moon Man.

The Youth Boxing League boys were gathered in the locker room at Barney's Gym, changing back into their street clothes after a morning workout. Paco waited until Angel was out of earshot, then leaned forward

"What've you got?"

and hissed, "Listen, you guys. Last night the Moon Man came to my place! He needs our help!"

Mickey stuck out his tongue and let fly a vigorous raspberry. "Pull the other one."

"No, for real," Paco insisted. "He found out about how we stopped those guys from hurting my pop."

The others stared at him, eyes wide.

"You ain't kidding?" T.J. ventured after a moment. "The real guy?"

"He came up the fire escape," Paco said with pride. "To my own window, swear to God. And he asked me to tell you guys to find out what's going on down at the docks. LeBaron's getting guns coming on a boat and the Moon Man's going to stop him. But he needs to know what boat."

"Shucks, that's easy," Isaac said. "My dad's a longshoreman. The ILA office has all that stuff on a list someplace when they give out the assignments in the morning. We could get a look at it."

"So what?" Josh snorted. "You think there's going to be something on it that says GUNS FOR FRANKIE? Be serious."

Isaac glared at him. "No, you dope. But we can figure it out. Guns are heavy and they come in crates. And everybody knows which warehouses LeBaron's guys use. So we look at the cargo manifests and we can eliminate stuff that's not going to those warehouses, and then we look at what's left and see which ones are the heavy loads."

Red added, "There's only about fifteen or twenty warehouses along the dock anyway. That ain't so hard. We just eliminate the impossible ones and search the offices of the ones what's left over."

"Like detectives!" Mickey was on board now, eyes alight at the thought of doing real detective work.

"But we gotta be careful," Paco added, almost as an afterthought. "I promised the Moon Man we would play it safe. He don't want anybody getting hurt."

"What's to hurt?" Isaac's tone was lofty. "It's just looking at papers in a buncha offices. How hard can that be?"

"Okay, then." Paco nodded. "We'll bring the outfits and suit up when we get to the docks."

All of them nodded. They scrambled to get dressed.

As the boys exited the gym out on to the street, each carrying his Moon Boy disguise wrapped in a gym towel, Paco thought, *This is great. We'll show the Moon Man we can be a real help to him.* The thought that they might be embarked on a very dangerous errand never entered his head.

Jonesy, the casino guard that was assigned to show Steve the ropes, turned out to be a very pleasant fellow, to Steve's mild surprise. He was a burly, balding man with a white fringe of hair circling the back of his head from ear to ear. He also had a neatly trimmed white mustache and beard, and blue eyes that sparkled with good humor. If he had been wearing a red suit, Steve thought, Jonesy would have looked almost like Santa Claus.

Instead, he was wearing a tweed jacket over a pale yellow dress shirt and dark brown slacks. The jacket was tailored to hide the .38 Marley that Jonesy was wearing in a shoulder rig under the left armpit. "Boss likes us to go heeled," he confided to Steve. "But to be honest I don't like using it. Never had a problem I couldn't handle with this." Jonesy pulled a small leather sap from his pocket with his right hand and lightly smacked it into his left. "Little tunk just behind the ear and the guy goes down like a sack of spuds. No muss, no fuss, and best of all, no murder rap hangin over ya. You never know if the fella causing trouble is somebody important. Some guy's kid or cousin or something."

Steve nodded. He was enjoying listening to Jonesy talk; the gunman had a knack for speaking easily without ever giving away anything important. It gave an illusion of indiscretion that Steve found amusing. He could almost admire the older man's attitude of easy professionalism. To hear Jonesy tell it, casino security for Frankie LeBaron was just a job, even if it occasionally involved handing out the occasional punitive beating... or worse, though Jonesy never outright admitted participating in anything illegal.

At the moment they were standing outside the door to the counting room. Four men in dark suits brushed past them, the one in the lead nodding briefly to Jonesy. Jonesy stepped back and motioned Steve to do the same. The man at the door rapped sharply, twice, once, twice. The door swung open and Steve had a brief glimpse of a white-tiled room with several women seated at a central table covered in stacks of cash. The door swung closed again with a quiet click.

"Wood veneer over steel," Jonesy said with an air of quiet pride. "And the walls are ten-inch concrete. Better'n a bank vault. Casinos don't screw around with security."

Steve nodded. He filed the information, and the code knock, away in the part of his brain that kept track of things that might be useful to the Moon Man. It would be nice to have a donation from Frankie LeBaron for the Southtown clinic before the undercover operation put him away.

Jonesy checked his watch and glanced up at LeBaron's office window overlooking the main floor. Steve looked up as well and saw LeBaron standing at the window. He crooked a finger.

"Boss wants something," Jonesy told Steve. "Back in a sec. Mind the guy over there by the craps table, Doris says he's been in a couple times this week with a load on and can't keep his hands to himself. We might have to escort him outside before she dumps her drinks tray down his pants and makes a scene."

Steve grunted agreement and Jonesy stepped over to the hall stairs. On his own for the moment, Steve looked around the gaming room, trying to note any other useful details. It was relatively quiet at the moment; the afternoon lull before the evening crowd came. The door to the counting room opened again and the four men in dark suits emerged, two of them carrying large metal cases. Steve nodded at them as they passed and then decided he couldn't pass up the opportunity. He waited a moment and then casually fell into step a few paces behind the one in the rear, trying to look as though he was embarked on a routine chore that was coincidentally taking him in the same direction.

He followed them to a rear hallway on the ground floor. There was a door at the end of the hallway that led to the outdoor parking lot and one of the men not encumbered with a case said, "Sit tight and I'll bring the car around." Steve paused and turned into a doorway halfway down the hall. It was a storage closet full of office supplies. Steve busied himself looking through the shelves of paper and envelopes, trying to look as though he had been dispatched to fetch something, but all his attention was focused on listening to the three men further down the hall.

"So how long we supposed to wait for the boat?" one said.

"Could be all night. So what? We're getting paid. We stay in the warehouse till the German shows. Bring a deck of cards."

"I ain't dumb enough to play cards with you again."

Warehouse. Boat. Cases of money from the counting room going out under guard. The guns are coming in tonight! Steve knew he had to somehow get word to Gil but then a wild idea seized him. If the Moon Man got to the warehouse first, took the cases of money out from under LeBaron's nose just as Gil and the police arrived, why, that would probably cover the clinic's expenses for the rest of the year. He could get Angel to meet him with the Moon Man gear.

That was the last thought he had. Steve felt a hot wet jolt of pain just behind his left ear and everything went black. He collapsed bonelessly to the floor.

Over him, Jonesy shook his head sadly and pocketed the leather sap.

Behind Jonesy was the taller of the two men that had been at the Garcia grocery. He shoved past Jonesy, knelt over Steve's prone body, and peeled off the phony mustache. "Toldja he was a phony. This is the cop that gave us the trouble yesterday."

"Damn shame," Jonesy said. His expression held genuine regret. "He seemed like a nice kid."

The Moon Boys, now dressed in their black sweaters and silver helmets and masks, huddled around the rear entrance to the Great City Fisheries storage yard. This was the fourth place they'd checked out and by this time they had it down to a routine. The warehouses faced out to the water, all in a row, and most of them had a designated pier facing the front entrance of each just across the asphalt roadway running along the shoreline. Isaac had led them to the alley behind the warehouses, away from the water. Each of the warehouse buildings had its own storage yard, full of freight containers and discarded wooden pallets, behind the building. There were a few of those pallets strewn along the alley as well. The storage yards were fenced off from the alley, of course, but most of the wooden fences were in disrepair and usually the Moon Boys could find a loose board they could pry away to gain entrance. Failing that, the boys discovered that if one up-ended a discarded pallet and stood it against the fence, the spaces between the pallet boards made a fine stepladder for scaling that fence. Once inside, it was a question of threading their way through a maze of piled crates, always staying in the shadows, to where they could sneak in to the warehouse building itself.

This was far easier than one would suspect. At night, most of the warehouses and their yards had a watchman or a couple of security guards on duty; but this was late afternoon, and everyone was working. That was the key, Isaac had explained. "All the action's out front, by the doors to the pier," he said. "Mornings are for bringing stuff in; afternoons, it's mostly crates going out to the boats. Nobody watches the back of the yard. We just gotta be quiet."

It had worked perfectly, except that the first three warehouses they'd checked out had proven to be innocent and largely deserted. Paco hoped this one would be the payoff; his visit from the Moon Man had galvanized him. He was feeling driven to prove his usefulness and something of this urgency had spread to the others as well.

The Great City Fisheries yard was proving to be a bit more of a challenge than the other warehouses. The fence was new and the back gate secured with a padlock, and even this part of the alley was tidy and free of pallets. "We could go back and bring one from one of the others," Josh suggested.

"Nah, we can climb it." Paco peered through a crack in the boards. "Over here, they got stuff piled on the other side. C'mon Mickey, I'll give you a boost."

Mickey nodded and, with Paco's help, scrambled up and over. His helmeted head bobbed up a moment later. "They got all the pallets stacked here," he said. "Hang on and I'll get one out there for you to climb up."

He disappeared again and then a flat wooden pallet scraped over the top of the fence, teetered, and then dropped into the alley. Instantly the boys picked it up and leaned it against the fence and soon the others were standing beside Mickey inside the yard, huddled in the shadow of a large freight container.

"Back door's locked too," Mickey said. He sighed. "This is a tough one."

T.J. pointed. "There's an upper window open. We could stack a couple of these pallets over there, lean one up against the wall, that would be enough for one of us to reach, wouldn't it? Then that one lets the others in. Mick, you're the smallest."

Mickey nodded, his round face looking grim under his improvised silver mask.

"All right," Paco agreed. "But be quiet. They got this place locked up so tight they must be nervous about something. And it ain't fish."

The six boys moved towards the warehouse wall, each carrying a wooden pallet. They stacked four of the pallets flat just underneath the open window, creating a platform about three feet high. Then they leaned the final two against the wall, one atop the other, to form a rickety sort of ladder that reached up another twelve feet to just brush the bottom of the window sill. T.J. and Josh stood on each side of this fragile arrangement and held it tightly in place, as well as bracing it with their bodies.

"Quick, Mickey," Josh hissed. "I don't know how long we can hold this."

Mickey nodded and clambered up the improvised ladder like a monkey. He peered in the window and then beckoned to the others. "Be careful," he said. "There's no second floor, it's just the rafters. It's probably why they left this one open."

"Can't you just get down and unlock the door from inside?" Red asked him.

"Not without making too much noise. They got some guys up in front.

Just sitting playing cards. That's weird." Mickey stiffened. "Aw jeez. They got a guy tied up! He's in a chair by the front."

"What? Mick, get outta the way, I'm coming up. Climb in and stand on a rafter or something." Mickey did so and Paco carefully picked his way up the stacked pallets. At one point he felt it shift a little but T.J. and Josh kept it from collapsing, and then Paco was over the sill. He looked at the scene in the warehouse and his eyes went wide. He leaned out the window and addressed the others. "It's that cop," he said. "The one that's friends with Mr. Angel. Guys, we gotta help him!"

"How?" Isaac was skeptical. "They got guns and we didn't load up on rocks this time."

"Call the cops?" Red ventured. "I mean, if it's one of their guys…"

"No cops," Paco said. "LeBaron owns every one that works the docks. They'll just kill him and dump him under a pier somewhere. No, we gotta tell Mr. Angel. He can get a message to the Moon Man." He thought a minute. "We don't all need to go. Okay, Mickey and me will stay and keep an eye on things. Josh and T.J. go find Mr. Angel, he probably is hanging around at the gym or the diner across the street. Isaac, you maybe go tell your dad? I dunno how deep Frankie's got his hooks in the ILW…"

"He ain't union," Isaac said. "I bet Dad could find some guys to help. They don't like Frankie any more'n we do."

"What about me?" Red asked.

"You scrounge us up something to use as a weapon," Paco said. "Since we didn't bring the baseball bats. Maybe some boards or a couple pieces of pipe."

"Gotcha." Red clearly liked the idea. "There was some pipe in the yard two buildings up."

"Okay then." Paco beckoned to Mickey. "You and me, we're gonna creep quiet as mice along the rafters to where those guys have Mr. Angel's friend. Maybe we can get him loose."

Steve awakened with only a mild headache. *Guess Jonesy wasn't kidding,* he reflected. *He really is an expert at 'thunking' people with that sap of his.*

He tried to move and found he couldn't. His arms and torso had been lashed to an old office chair. His feet and legs were free, but he saw it would do him little good, since a few feet away he saw the four men in suits he had followed earlier gathered around a flat-top desk, playing cards. They had discarded their suit jackets and he saw that all four were wearing guns in shoulder holsters. Steve thought ruefully that it must have been the house uniform and cursed his own caution in coming to the casino absolutely clean. He'd thought he might have to stand for a frisk and didn't want the added headache of explaining why he'd come armed to a job interview, but now he was wishing he'd had the forethought to carry some kind of a weapon. Say, a knife in a forearm sheath. That would certainly have come in handy in this situation. As it was he only had his wits.

Well, all right, put those wits to use. Where was he? The room was large and dark, with only a small overhead light from a hanging bulb a few feet over the card game. Concrete floor. Vague squared-off shapes in the shadows that looked like stacked crates surrounding them on all sides. And he could smell that industrial port smell, the vague combination of rotting algae and machine oil that meant he was near the docks. So he was in LeBaron's warehouse. *Damn it, to be so close… This is what I went undercover to dig out. The big gun buy's tonight. If only I could get word to Gil!*

He heard a door open and close. Then LeBaron himself entered the dimly lit room from behind a stack of crates. The others dropped their cards and shifted as if to rise, but LeBaron waved them away. "It's fine, fellas." He moved over to where Steve sat tied in his chair and regarded him with his heavy-lidded gaze for a long moment.

"So," LeBaron said, finally. "Not from Chicago. Tony says you're a badge. You local, shamus?"

Steve thought maybe he could run a bluff. "Part of a special task force," he said. "We're looking to take down the Chicago families. Ness and Capone was just the beginning. You know we got Marucci last week and Bartell's going to hand us a bunch more of your friends. You bought yourself a big piece of trouble when you got in bed with the mob, Frankie. My people are on their way here, probably right now. Get me out of this and maybe you could cut a deal."

LeBaron let out one of his humorless barks of laughter. "You got sand, shamus. But I think you are blowing a lot of smoke. I got guys on the force. They tell me who's in town looking to stir up trouble for guys like me. There ain't no special task force looking for me. I'm small potatoes. But not for much longer."

"Because you have German munitions coming in tonight by ship. Guns for the Chicago mob. You hook up Paul Ricci and his friends with major-league hardware, they'll have to let you sit at the big-boy table. That's the plan, Frankie?"

LeBaron spread his hands. "So I have ambition. Why not? It's just business. Somebody's going to deal with them. Why not me?"

"So you scare Southtown business owners into donating their hard-earned money to your business expansion. Threatening their wives and families. Because you have *ambition*." Steve's voice dripped with contempt.

LeBaron shrugged off Steve's outrage. "The big fish eat the little fish, shamus. That's just nature." The casino owner turned back to the men at the table. "What time is it?"

"Coming up on nine-thirty," one of the card players replied. "You want we should do something about this guy?" He nodded at Steve.

LeBaron shook his head. "No time. This is fine for now. I need you guys here for the loading and I don't want to deal with getting rid of a body, and anyway, we don't need the heat from a cop-killing. We'll figure something out later. I'm trying to get this deal done. Boat'll be here in a half-hour." He moved over to the group playing cards, dismissing Steve.

Unobtrusively, while LeBaron's back was to him, Steve tested his bonds. No give in them at all. If he was going to get loose, someone was going to have to cut those cords off him. His legs were free and the office chair was on rollers, but the thought of trying to scuttle towards an exit while still bound was ludicrous; there were so many crates piled around him and the light was so bad that he wasn't even sure where the exit was. He sighed. His only hope, and it was a pretty slim hope, was that LeBaron's reluctance to murder a police officer would keep him safe long enough that eventually Steve would have a chance to make some kind of a move. He would just have to wait and be ready.

Suddenly Steve noticed something odd. There was some kind of movement above, in the rafters. He squinted and for a second he thought he saw a small figure crawling along the main beam, and a glint of silver. It was hard to see anything up there because of the hanging bulb of the light, but... no. There was definitely a person up there. In silver headgear and mask. The Moon Boys? Here?

There was a stealthy rustle of clothing behind him. "Mister, roll back about a foot and a half. I got a pocketknife. I can cut you loose." It was Paco's voice.

"You kids shouldn't be here," Steve whispered. "You were supposed to stay out of trouble."

"You want we should leave you tied up?"

The kid had a point, and anyway Steve knew that if he tried to carry on a whispered conversation LeBaron and his boys would be on to them.

Slowly and silently, he rolled the chair back to where the back of the chair was almost into an aisle between two stacks of large wooden crates. "Cut me loose and then you and your friends need to get the hell out of here and go find some help."

"Okay, mister." He could feel Paco sawing away at the cords.

Then it all went to hell. There was a squawk of dismay from above and a silver-helmeted figure fell awkwardly past the hanging light to land with a painful thump atop the desk. Playing cards went everywhere. The men leaped to their feet, guns drawn. LeBaron stepped forward and lifted the Moon Boy by the scruff of the neck with no more visible effort than he would have with a kitten. He dangled the boy in front of him and snarled, "Who the hell are you?"

Under his mask, Mickey's eyes glared with anger. He said two words, the second of which was "you." LeBaron's face went red with rage and he shook the boy angrily.

One of the gunmen said, "It's those Moon kids what got Vito and Tony yesterday!" He pointed his gun at Mickey. "Boss, I say we blow a hole in this punk right now."

The cords parted. Steve didn't wait but launched himself at the gunman who was about to take a shot at Mickey and they went down in a tangle of arms and legs. Paco followed and instantly two of the guns were trained on him. He skidded to a halt and raised his hands.

Steve was still struggling with the man on the floor when he felt the cold steel of a gun muzzle on his neck. "That's enough," came LeBaron's voice. "Stop and get up with your hands in the air or I shoot these two kids. Mike, Pete, go find out if there's any others around someplace."

Steve sighed and let the other man up. The hoods lined Steve up with the two boys against a large crate. LeBaron stepped forward and lifted off the homemade silver helmets from the boys' heads, then tore off the masks. Paco and Mickey glared back at him, red-faced and panting.

"Who sent you?" LeBaron asked. "Do you work for the Moon Man?"

Mickey blew a raspberry. Paco said, "We ain't afraid of you."

This amused LeBaron. "Really? Because you should be. Keep an eye on them," he told the others. "I'm going out front to meet the boat. Any of them gives you any trouble, shoot them."

"Why not just shoot them now?" growled the one Steve had tackled. Clearly he held a grudge.

"I don't want a bunch of guns going off in here while I make my deal with the Germans. I can't let them think we don't know how to do things here. Just keep 'em on ice." LeBaron moved off.

"Do you work for the Moon Man?"

Steve's heart sank. Not only had he blown his one chance, but now these two kids were going to pay the price for it.

Angel Dargan was worried. Sue knew it was true because the waitress had brought Angel's ham and eggs fifteen minutes ago and he had barely touched them. Normally when they ate at the diner Angel vacuumed up his breakfast in five minutes or less.

Sue was worried too, but she was determined not to let it get the best of her. She smiled at Angel. "Come on, it's only been a day."

"I know." Angel's voice was gloomy. "I just don't like him being in there without any backup at all. It's one thing playing cat-and-mouse with cops when he's the Moon Man. Your dad talks tough but I don't think he'd just gun Steve down in cold blood, he has rules. But Frankie and his boys don't play by no rules. And you know how many crazy chances the boss takes."

"Believe me, I know." Sue sighed. "That's why I called. I thought maybe you'd be willing to be my date tonight if we looked in at the casino. Just check in, see how Steve's holding up."

"Hey now!" Angel brightened. "You think he'd mind? I wouldn't want to joggle his elbow or nothing, but…"

"Of course he'll mind." Sue sniffed. "But on our account, not on his own. So what? I get the *stay out of danger, you shouldn't take risks* lecture once or twice a week anyway. As if I'm the one that puts a fishbowl on my head and goes out to clean up Great City. This way we'll be around if he needs us. We'll just hang around and play some blackjack or something for a couple of hours. If he waves us off we'll come home. But at least we'd know how he's doing."

Angel nodded. "All right. I'll bring the satchel with the Moon Man gear along, just in case." At Sue's grimace, he added, "Look, you know as well as I do that Steve took this on because he was thinking of getting some LeBaron cash for the clinic. He might have hatched a plan by now."

"I know," Sue sighed. "But still…hey, isn't that one of your boys?"

T.J. had entered the diner. He looked around rather wildly and when he saw Angel and Sue, he sprinted for them. "Mister Angel, ma'am, you gotta come with me, we got trouble. Your friend, the man that was with this lady in the gym yesterday, he's in a jam."

"I knew it," Sue muttered darkly.

Angel nodded at T.J. to sit down. "All right, T.J. Take a breath and settle down. Start at the beginning."

T.J. nodded. He told them the whole story, beginning with the Moon Man's visit to Paco and ending with their visit to the warehouse, and Paco's decision to stay behind with Mickey.

Throughout this recitation, Sue's face grew progressively whiter. "It was Steve? You're sure?" she demanded when T.J. finished.

T.J. nodded. "Yes ma'am. I think Paco was gonna try and get him loose. And Isaac went to go get his dad, he thinks the union guys might help."

"Of course he did. Because God forbid anyone call a cop." Sue stood up. "There's a pay phone in the back, Angel. I'm calling Dad."

Angel nodded. "Do that," he said. "Tell him to bring the whole squad with him. But give me a twenty-minute head start, Sue. Please. You know why. T.J., you're with me, there's some gear I need to pick up."

Sue hesitated, then nodded. "All right, Angel. But don't take any silly chances."

"I think that ship sailed already," Angel said with a rueful grin. "All right, T.J. I'm picking up a bag at the gym and then you're going to show me where this warehouse is."

At the warehouse, LeBaron had taken three of the men with him out to the pier, leaving just one to stand guard over Steve and the boys. Steve knew he'd never get a better chance… if he could just distract the guy for a moment. They probably didn't have more than a minute or two at the most. Any second the big doors would open and LeBaron's men would start bringing crates in.

Then there was some kind of commotion out front. "The hell is this?" Steve heard a man shout. "Using scab labor to bring in cargo at night? What the hell kind of operation you running here?"

Paco elbowed Steve. "That's Isaac's dad!" he whispered.

Steve nodded. He hissed, "When I move, you boys run. Home. As fast as you can, get me? Don't try and be heroes."

Before the boys could respond, there was a rustle from above, and a length of lead pipe about a foot long flew down and hit LeBaron's gunman in the head. Steve didn't wait to see who threw it, but launched himself in a flat, hard dive at the thug's waistline. The impact carried both of them tumbling back and the thug's head hit the side of the steel office desk with a sharp crack. Steve rolled off him and raised a fist, but there was no need. The impact with the desk had been plenty. The gunman slumped to the floor, unconscious.

Steve scooped up the gunman's pistol from the floor. A figure dropped from the rafters, grinning wide under the silver mask and helmet.

"Red!" Mickey blurted.

The Moon Boy nodded. "I just had to wait till the others went outside," he said, almost shyly. "I knew there'd only be one shot at hitting one of them."

Steve nodded. "You boys have done more than enough. On your way, now. Out the back."

"What about you?" Paco said.

"I'm right behind you. But I've got to take care of something first." Fate, and the boys, had given him a second chance to put a stop to LeBaron's plans and Steve wasn't going to waste it. No time to call Gil and get a police unit down here. He had to make some kind of play right now before one of those union guys got a bullet in him. Gun at the ready, he started for the front, when an urgent whispered hiss came from behind him.

"Boss!" It was Angel Dargan, carrying a satchel.

Steve's jaw dropped in astonishment. "How the hell…?"

"The boys came and found me. Sue's right behind me with Gil and a squad of police. We don't have long." Angel held out the satchel. "But I figured you might want to get a donation from LeBaron before we hand him to the cops."

"You bet I do." Steve grinned. He opened the satchel and removed his Moon Man helmet and cape. "Nicely done, Angel. Now get those boys out of here."

"I already sent 'em to the car, it's in the alley behind. You sure you don't need my help?" Angel looked a little worried.

"No, you go on. I want those kids out of danger." Steve had donned his helmet and cloak and gloves. Now it was the Moon Man that pointed at the rear of the warehouse. "I can handle LeBaron. Get a move on."

"Okay." Angel was reluctant but knew better than to argue. He disappeared into the darkness between the crates. Threading his way through the shadows, he emerged out into the storage yard and quickly made his way to where the other boys were waiting. "Over the fence and into the car, fellas… hey. Where's Paco?"

Frankie LeBaron's evening had been getting steadily worse. First the cop, then the damn Moon kids, and now this union crap. He spread his hands. "Now look," he said. "My business is my business, gentlemen. This is a private warehouse."

The burly union man standing in front of him was having none of it. He pointed at the small trawler that had just pulled up to the pier. Two German sailors had just finished mooring it to the dock with a couple of big hawsers and now they were lowering a gangplank. "This is not how we do things here," he said. "At night? Using scab labor? You guys are acting like bootleggers. Fisheries my ass."

There was a mutter of angry agreement from the three other longshoremen behind the union man. LeBaron sighed. "All right then, we'll do it the hard way." He gestured at his men and immediately they had their guns out and trained on the longshoremen.

"Here's how it works tonight," LeBaron said. "You men go home now and forget this ever happened. Or your bodies'll be feeding the fishes out in the bay there."

The longshoremen looked at one another and then started to back slowly away. "This isn't over," the one in front said. "We'll be back with more guys."

"If you come back you'll regret it. Apparently you need a demonstration." LeBaron turned to his men. "Shoot one of them, Pete. I don't care which."

A shot rang out. Pete collapsed.

The other men all whirled to see a cloaked figure in a silver helmet step out from the warehouse. "Frankie, you and your boys are covered. You other gentlemen should go home."

"The Moon Man!" blurted one of the longshoremen. "Jesus, he's as bad as the…"

The Moon Man waved his pistol. "Yes, I'm a very bad man," he said pleasantly. "All the papers say so and I don't have time to argue. Get out of here."

The four longshoremen broke and ran. The Moon Man gestured at the two Germans on the gangplank. "You boys, you just put that back and sail on out of here. No sale."

They hesitated.

The Moon Man fired and a bullet kicked up splinters a foot from where the Germans were standing. "Next one goes into the leg," he said. "Now move. I want to see you on your way with steam up in two minutes."

The German sailors moved with alacrity. They were back on board their ship in moments, and had cast off the moorings a second later.

When the trawler was steaming out towards the middle of the bay, the Moon Man said, "Now that it's just us, Frankie, we can talk business. There are two suitcases of money inside that warehouse. I want them."

LeBaron's composure finally broke. This was all he could take. He spluttered, "Like hell, you freak," and whipped out his own pistol.

But it's impossible to outdraw a man who already has a gun trained on you. The Moon Man fired once, twice, three times. LeBaron screamed and dropped his gun, clutching his wounded thigh. Behind him, two of the gunmen collapsed as well, writhing in pain from the wounds the Moon Man's other two shots had inflicted; one in the upper arm, the other with a shattered knee. The Moon Man gestured at the one left standing, who was gaping at the helmeted figure in disbelieving horror. "Pick up those guns, junior…no, by the barrel, that's right, and throw them in the water. There you go. Now, we'll have to…"

The wail of a police siren cut him off. Two black-and-whites were approaching, red lights flashing. The Moon Man shrugged. "Another time, Frankie," he said, and ran for the warehouse just as the first of the black-and-whites skidded to a halt on the pier and Gil McEwen leaped out.

"Halt! Damn you!" McEwen bawled.

The Moon Man disappeared into the warehouse. Gil gestured to the uniformed officers with him. "Cuff all of those guys, and get them to a hospital. I'm going after that bastard in the helmet." He sprinted for the warehouse.

McEwen found the warehouse deserted, but the door to the back of the storage yard was open. He thought he saw a silhouetted figure in a silver helmet moving out in the yard and screamed, "Halt!" again. The silhouette kept moving and Gil fired, twice.

The silhouette collapsed. Gil emerged into the blue moonlight of the storage yard to find a fifteen-year-old Mexican kid sprawled at his feet, bleeding from wounds in the arm and thigh. Next to him was a silver football helmet.

"My God," Gil whispered. "Oh, Jesus, no."

The Moon Man emerged from behind a pile of scrap iron. Instantly McEwen's pistol was up again and aimed at the man in the helmet. "This is your fault," he said.

"Yes. I know." The Moon Man's shoulders slumped.

The flat admission of guilt took Gil McEwen by surprise. "You're covered," he said, as the Moon Man knelt to examine the unconscious boy. "Step away from him and raise your hands."

"He's still breathing," the Moon Man said. "We need to get him to a hospital. That's what I'm going to do."

"I'll see to his care," snapped McEwen. "You aren't going anywhere."

"You'd see to his care in prison. I'm not going to let you ruin this boy's life because he had the misfortune to run afoul of your obsession with me." The Moon Man dropped his pistol to the ground and scooped Paco up in his arms. "I'm unarmed now. You can't prove I've committed any crime here tonight. So I'm leaving now, with the boy. You can stop me, but you'll have to shoot me to do it. I don't think you're the kind of cop that will shoot an unarmed man in the back." He paused. "In fact, I'm betting my life on it."

The cloaked figure slung the boy over his shoulder and made for a pile of stacked crates leaning against the back fence. Gil McEwen watched him go.

"I'm an idiot," he muttered.

Then the caped man was over the fence. Gil heard a car ignition roar to life. *License number, at least,* he thought, and ran for the crates. He scrambled up to the top of the fence just in time to see a pair of red taillights disappearing into the distance. Too dark to see even the make of the car, let alone the license. He heard a groan and looked down to see Steve Thatcher sitting up, rubbing his forehead. "Steve? Are you all right?"

"Just a headache. Somebody clobbered me and dumped me back here." Steve flashed Gil a rueful smile. "Looks like I missed some excitement."

"We have to check all the area hospitals," Gil McEwen was saying two days later, in the waiting room of the Southtown clinic. "It's procedure. That boy might be our only lead to the Moon Man."

"But Dad..." Sue McEwen's eyes flashed with anger. "This isn't a hospital! It's a walk-in clinic for sick kids. I volunteer here all the time and I can assure you there's nothing shady going on." She waved an all-encompassing hand around them at the waiting room full of women and children. "There's nothing more sinister here than the sniffles. I can't have you tearing up the place looking for gangsters. Why don't you go some place where some real criminals are?"

"Now, don't be mad," McEwen said. "I had to check, that's all. Your word's good enough. Home for dinner?"

"Around seven, probably." Sue smiled. "Go on with you, now. I have work to do."

Gil nodded, tipped his hat at the throng in the waiting room, and left.

As soon as Sue was sure he was gone she spun and trotted down the hallway to a treatment room in the back, where a bed was curtained off.

She pulled back the curtain to reveal Paco lying in bed, with Angel and Steve standing nearby.

"Mission accomplished," she said. "I hope you boys are happy."

Steve pulled her to him. "You did great. That was my only worry. I knew Dr. Sandoval would play ball but I was sure your dad would want a check on all the area hospitals. ...and nobody else could have made him leave without a search."

"I know." Sue grimaced. "I'm probably going to hell."

"But you'll be in good company." Steve hugged her and she smiled up at him.

Paco stirred and waved drowsily at the three of them. "Hey, you guys," he said. "How you doing?"

"How are you doing, hero?" Steve grinned at the boy. "You're the one everybody owes."

"Wha-huh?" Paco blinked.

"Those cases you grabbed," Angel explained. "When you doubled back to the warehouse and almost gave me a heart attack. The ones you got shot over. Remember?"

"Kinda," Paco admitted. "It's blurry. I went back in because I didn't want to leave the helmets and masks, I thought maybe the cops would get fingerprints or something. And then I saw the cases and I realized about the money, Steve said it was from the neighborhood. So I took that too. I remember throwing them over the fence. But then..."

"Then a policeman shot you," Steve said. "The Moon Man got you out and brought you here."

"Oh God!" Paco sat up straight. "How long have I been...my mama and papa..."

"They're fine," Angel assured him. "They're packing."

Paco blinked again. "Packing?"

"For Phoenix," Steve explained. "Those cases you saved from the warehouse. There was over six hundred thousand dollars there. Plenty to reimburse the neighborhood businesses and make a donation to the clinic here, and enough left to set your folks up in a nice place down south. The doctor says that the Arizona climate should make things a lot easier for your mama."

Paco's eyes started to well up. "I don't know what to say," he mumbled. "I didn't..."

"You don't have to say anything." Steve laid a hand on his shoulder. "You and your friends saved my life. You stopped a big crime and you helped a lot of people. You should be proud of that."

Paco nodded, accepting it. "But… I'm not in trouble? What kind of cop are you, man?"

"The grateful kind." Steve shrugged. "I have real crooks to chase. This Moon Boys business was a crazy stunt and if you were my kid I'd probably tan your hide. But it all worked out. I don't see any need to bring police trouble down on you and your family. They're going to need you anyway. Lots of things to do to get ready for Arizona."

They turned to go, but a word from Paco stopped them. "Officer? I have a question."

"Yeah?" Steve looked at Sue and Angel. "Go ahead, I'll catch up." He moved back to Paco's bedside. "Well? What's your question?"

"In the warehouse," Paco said slowly. "You were mad at me for being there."

"It was a dangerous and stupid thing to do," Steve said. "You got two bullets put into you and even at that, you were very lucky. If you think…"

"No sir." Paco fell back into his pillows. He was tiring quickly. "But when you said that, when you were mad… that meant you knew right away who we were and you knew I promised the Moon Man we'd be safe. And then Angel showed up and the Moon Man was there too, but he didn't come in the car. I asked the guys."

"Uh huh." Steve kept his expression carefully blank.

"So, I was wondering… if you're a cop… then how can you be…?"

"Let's just stop right there." Steve smiled, a little thinly. "You serious about helping the Moon Man?"

Paco nodded.

"Then let's leave that one alone. It's best not to talk about it. Some day I'll visit you out in Arizona and tell you the whole story. I promise. In the meantime, well… you better get some rest. Your folks are going to need you to get well soon."

Paco nodded again, slower this time, and closed his eyes. In moments he was asleep.

Steve drew the curtain gently back to the closed position it had been in before and left.

Outside, Angel and Sue were waiting for him on the sidewalk. "Forgot to catch you up," Steve told them. "Found out this morning. Frankie and his boys are going down for that scene on the dock. D.A.'s office is holding them based on the testimony of Isaac's father and his union friends. Maybe we can show them that sometimes the police really do their job."

"Not much of a charge," Angel observed.

"Attempted murder," Steve said. "It's enough of a felony to get warrants to examine the warehouse office and go through those records, and they'll turn up evidence of Frankie's gun operation. That added to what Bartell's giving the Feds about Chicago's connections here in Great City was enough to get them to move on it. LeBaron's empire is coming down. Somebody else'll be along to replace him soon enough, but in the meantime, Southtown businesses can breathe easier." He paused. "How are your boys?"

"I think they figured out that maybe the Moon Man stuff is best left to the Moon Man," Angel said. "Packing Paco into the sedan with him bleeding all over the place spooked 'em. They were so worried they never even noticed your little switcheroo."

"I wouldn't want to cut it that close again." Steve chuckled. "Gil was barely a half-step from the fence when I shoved the cape and helmet under the dumpster and flopped. But it ended up being a safe enough place, the gear was waiting there for me the next morning."

"Why not? No need to search the alley." Angel grimaced. "Well, I gotta be on my way. Deliveries," he added. "Got about four more stores to visit with donations from LeBaron. Can I give you two a lift anyplace?"

"We'll walk, thanks. Too nice a day."

Angel nodded and raised a hand in salute before stepping to the sedan he had parked at the curb.

"So what was that all about with Paco?" Sue asked him after they had said goodbye to Angel. "What was the question?"

"He was wondering what kind of cop I was."

"Him and everyone else." Sue let out a distinctly unladylike snort. "You took an insane chance with Dad. You know that, right?"

"I knew what I was doing." Steve grinned. "I've worked with your dad a long time. He's the best police officer I know. He believes in the law. I was betting on that and I won."

Sue slitted her eyes and gave him a hard look. "And you? What do you believe in, Steve? What kind of cop are you?"

Steve laughed. "I'm the kind of cop that can trust his friends. That's what I believe in. The people I have around me. That's all either of us needs, really; Steve or the Moon Man." And with that, he pulled her to him and kissed her.

THE END

AFTERWORD

For me, with the Moon Man it's all about getting past the helmet.

I originally encountered Steve Thatcher and his alter ego in a book called *Tough Guys and Dangerous Dames*, a wonderful hardcover collection of old pulp detective yarns. It reprinted his initial outing, "The Sinister Sphere," and most of the elements that made up the fun of the series were there from the get-go—the tension between Steve's daytime life as a cop and his nocturnal activity as a vigilante, the secret-identity problems he had to deal with given that his partner Gil McEwen was obsessed with the Moon Man's capture, and most of all, the determination Steve Thatcher had to bring some fairness and justice to the families being crushed by the Great Depression.

And, of course, the fishbowl-and-cape costume the Moon Man wears. Realistically, it's pretty unwieldy, but to his credit author Frederick C. Davis took that problem head-on (so to speak) in the very first story and made it work. So I tried to respect that when I wrote this one. There's a certain amount of "just go with it" that plays into every pulp-hero story, after all, and Davis was so thorough in setting up everything else and making it plausible that I kind of have to give the outfit a pass.

So I did my best to embrace the Moon Man's world and work with what Fred Davis had initially set up. And as it turned out this story ended up being quite a bit more personal for me than I'd originally thought it would.

See, when I'm not writing pulp fiction, I teach writing and art classes for seventh and eighth-grade kids as part of an after-school arts program. For the last couple of summers I've been involved in something called the "Level Nine" program, essentially a bridge for students from middle school to high school. The idea is to shore up their academic skills and give them a little bit of a leg up on high school, which can be a really intimidating prospect for a lot of students.

The Level Nine program I was involved with required working with what is euphemistically referred to as "at-risk youth," in what one would call a "bad neighborhood." During the time I spent teaching there I was struck by how *acclimated* to street crime the kids were; all of them knew which corners the drug dealers were working, where the crack houses were, what streets to avoid. The police were apparently oblivious, but any twelve-year-old could tell you where to buy heroin. It was as natural to them as the weather, it permeated their lives. The ongoing battle we had as teachers was to somehow persuade our students that there was a better way to live than dropping out of school and selling dope, despite the fact that the kids saw their older brothers and sisters making hundreds of dollars a day doing exactly that.

One of the ways I found to encourage students was to let them tell their own stories, in prose and comics. And again, street crime permeated their creative efforts. Stories of robbery and killing and doomed romance, stories of kids trying to reach for something higher and getting slapped down, stories of hopelessness and rage. They were taking the anger at their situation and putting it all on the page. I was incredibly proud of them, but I also found myself getting angry on their behalf. So many of them were hungering for a fair chance. Not a handout, but just a *chance*, the opportunity to compete on a level playing field. To have the same shot at college and a decent life that rich white kids did.

Not only that, but my wife recently took a job as house supervisor at a teenage drug and alcohol rehab facility. The stories she brings home about the boys she works with are rife with the same kind of rage-fueled desperation, of kids looking for some way out of a bad situation.

These were all things I was thinking of when I sat down to write this story. Once you get past the fishbowl helmet, there's a dark, cynical, *noir* tone to the original Moon Man stories. Steve Thatcher is usually caught between what's right and what's legal, and his determination to make things better for the poor of Great City often blows up in his face. So thinking about that, and about the very real challenges faced by young people living in the urban poverty of the Depression, is what sparked the idea of the Moon Boys. I wanted Steve to have to deal with unintended consequences—one of the reasons pulp heroes adopt a costumed identity in the first place is to be an inspiration to others, and I liked the notion of Steve being forced to acknowledge that isn't always a good thing. And I wanted to honor Fred Davis' original idea about putting Steve's responsibilities as a policeman in direct collision with his other identity as the Moon Man.

As always, I ended up doing a fair amount of research. The Moon Man operated during the Great Depression, which puts his adventures squarely in the early 1930s. I found myself reading about the tuberculosis epidemic that raged through big cities—it was so common that at one point one in four deaths was attributed to TB, or 'consumption' as it was commonly referred to. And it was particularly lethal in poor neighborhoods. No cure existed until the discovery of antibiotics, which I was surprised to learn didn't happen until the late 1930s—and streptomycin, the most common prescription for TB, didn't exist until 1946. At the time of this story, the only treatment available was bed rest and relocating to a dry climate, which was out of reach for most of the working poor.

I also spent some time looking into the way the Chicago mobs worked in the 1930s, and the whole vice machine that originally sprang into being as a support system for the speakeasies during the Prohibition era. Pete Ricci, who's name-checked in the preceding story, was a real guy—he took over the Chicago machine after Capone and Nitti were sent up. The casino operation as described is one of several systems in use at the time. (My original idea was to have the Moon Man somehow engineer an actual casino heist but the plain fact is that it simply would not have been possible for one man, even a pulp superhero.)

Of course, there's the adventure element too. Being socially conscious and trying to write something realistic about the working poor doesn't mean I'm not in the business of doing pulp adventure. One of the things I was trying to bring to this was the swashbuckling action vibe I remembered from young-adult fiction writers like Jim Lawrence and Robert Arthur—there's a lot of *The Three Investigators* in the Moon Boys. Arthur, especially, had the knack of bringing warmth and humor to his youthful protagonists while at the same time making sure they played for real stakes.

That's about all I have to say about where this one came from; all that's left are the thank-yous. I am greatly indebted to Edward Wozniak at *Balladeer's Blog,* who has very helpfully indexed all the Moon Man stories online; I couldn't have done this without that as a reference. I also appreciate my first-reader crew, who as always had helpful feedback and suggestions: Anne Hawley, Sena Friesen, Brekke Ferguson, Lorinda Adams, Ed Bosnar, and Tiffany Tomcal. And of course my wife Julie, without whom I'd be useless at most things, let alone writing.

But most of all, I appreciate my students in the Level Nine summer program who inspired this story in the first place. Fernando, Lisette, Haley, Juan, Jennifer, Ulysses, Huang, Mike, Angelo, and Lynn, this one's for you.

GREG HATCHER - is a writer and teacher from Seattle, Washington. In addition to the aforementioned Level Nine summer classes, he teaches both Cartooning and Young Authors as part of an afterschool arts program created through the YMCA's Partners With Youth. He was a contributing editor at With Magazine for over a decade where he won several awards for both fiction and non-fiction pieces, and currently writes a weekly column for the Comics Should Be Good! blog for the Atomic Junk Shop. He lives in an apartment in south Seattle with his wife Julie, their cat Maggie, and roughly ten thousand books and comics.

THE FACELESS TERROR

By Tim Holter Bruckner

*I*t was the single most important event in Great City's history. Anyone who was anyone was going to try and be there. *Try*, being the operative work. Tickets were limited. If you signed up early, you were lucky. If you signed up late and had an extra wheel barrow or two full of cash, and knew someone who knew someone, your chances got a little better. Aside from those two options you were out of luck.

The Mayor and his wife were coming, of course. Several councilmen and their wives were on the list. The chief of Police, Peter Thatcher and the Head of Detectives, Lieutenant Gilbert "Gil" McEwen and his daughter Susan, were both a must show.

Miriam Hopkins, Kay Francis and Herbert Marshall were scheduled to fly in from Hollywood that afternoon and Ernie Hare and Billie Jones of the Happiness Boys radio show were also scheduled to appear.

The event was being held in the Great City Grand Ballroom, recently restored after a fire that nearly burnt it to the ground the year before. The Saint Anne's Children's Hospital Gala was hoping to raise enough money to build and outfit a new pediatric cancer wing. It was to rival the best and to attract the best; doctors, nurses and researchers that would put Great City on the map as a center for cutting edge medical care. If everything went according to plan, they would reach their goal and then some.

Sue McEwen, daughter of the Lieutenant, and Sister Mary Catherine, Mother Superior of the Sisters of Mercy, had been planning, organizing and working around the clock the past eighteen months to make the event a success.

It was a clear night. The threat of rain had been defeated by a steady breeze that rolled the clouds out into the foothills. The full moon was so bright and yellow; it looked like an October lantern hung from a cluster of twinkling stars against a midnight blue background. Town cars lined the street as far as the eye could see. Two klieg lights crisscrossed the sky as teams of newsreel reporters elbowed one another to get film of the famous and near famous walking the red carpet to the two grand polished bronze doors. Flashbulbs popped so fast and furious, it felt like the Fourth of July.

"Ain't this something?" Detective Stephen Thatcher said as he and Sue skirted the crowd heading toward the rear entrance. "You know, it should be you on that red carpet."

She smiled and gave him a kiss on the cheek. "Aw heck," she said. "I'm not anybody."

He stopped and turned her to look at him, "Nobody, eh?" he said, looking into her soft brown eyes. "If it wasn't for you this whole shebang wouldn't even be happening. Sister is a swell dame and all, but she couldn't organize a fire brigade."

"Now, Stephen, that's not fair," Sue said defensively. "Sister Mary Catherine has worked as hard if not harder than me to get this thing going."

"Who got them movie stars here? And those radio boys?" Stephen pursued. "And all the stuff for the raffle?"

She blushed and looked down at his vest buttons.

"Who got those newsreel boys, and the society reporters covering that red carpet," he said jabbing his thumb over his shoulder, "like it was some big time Hollywood movie premiere? If it wasn't for you Suzanne Margaret McEwen, the hospital would be lucky to get a new thermometer and a mustard plaster."

She laughed.

"I sure am proud of you, Sue. I sure am," and leaned in and kissed her.

From back stage, looking out into the ballroom, it was like a scene from some highfalutin fairy tale. A sea of white draped tables adorned with hundreds of flickering blue glass candle holders. A mirror ball hung from the center of the ceiling sending a cascade of floating stars up the walls and across the floor as if the whole room was suspended in a nighttime sky.

The band was playing *Fascination* as the guests arrived and were escorted to their tables. Sister Mary Catherine spotted the couple standing just at the edge of the stage curtain and beamed at them.

"You know," Sue began, "Sister's niece has cancer."

Stephen turned to look at her.

"No, I didn't" Stephen said. "Is it bad?"

She gave his hand a squeeze as she smiled and blew a kiss to Sister Mary across the room.

There were lots of introductions. There were so many handshakes and kissed cheeks, Sue was starting to get a little worn out and the evening wasn't even half over.

"What you need is a nice glass of champagne," Stephen suggested and sat her down at a table near the stage door as he went to get them each a glass of the bubbly.

There was a commotion at the Ballroom doors, some kind of scuffle. Stephen turned to see three men enter. There was an average-sized man flanked by two guys so massively tall that he looked like a toddler being escorted to school by his parents. The band stopped playing. The entire ballroom went quiet as the three strode to the first row of tables. The giants wore oddly tailored black suits and small, wide-brimmed hats. Each held a Tommy gun in their ham-hock hands, and moved them from side to side, watching, alert like panthers on the prowl.

The man in the center of these two goons was dressed in a suit of deep red. It was cut in the same oddly antique style as his bodyguards. He wore a high collared knee length cape of the same dark red fabric lined with black velvet. Stephen blinked several times and rubbed his fists into his eyes. He could not be seeing what he was seeing. The man had no face. There was a vague sense of a hairline and shadowy shapes that could have been ears. But his face was a void of undulating shadows. Set in that nothingness were two narrowed eyes that glowed red and hot as hardwood embers. They actually seemed to give off heat.

"Please, ladies and gentlemen," the faceless man said in a slight accent. "Do not move. This is a robbery. If you would all leave your tables in a calm and orderly fashion and line up against the wall, my friends and I will relieve you of your belongings, one by one."

At first, nobody moved. Then bit by bit, tables emptied and guests walked slowly to the wall to which he pointed.

"There are law enforcement agents here," he said, stating a fact. "I would encourage you to fight your natural instinct. Is the death of any one of these fine people worth a misguided show of civic duty or overzealous bravery? I think not."

When all the guests had left their tables and were lined up against the wall, one of the goons walked to the center of the room, slowly moving his machine gun back and forth, watchful for the slightest errant move.

The faceless man, followed closely by his bodyguard, walked to the head of the line where Jason Morby and his wife Alice, both well into their sixties, were standing. Alice shook so terribly from fear and anxiety, Jason had to hold her tightly to him worried she might collapse. As the faceless man approached, the goon shouldered his gun and withdrew a black bag about double the size of a pillow case. He held it open, waiting.

"Your jewelry," the faceless man said to Alice, "and your wallet and watch," to Jason.

Both complied nervously, handing their valuables over. He examined them, admiring Alice's diamond bracelet and then dropped them into the bag.

One by one, he went down the line. When he got to Gil McEwen, he stopped, looking the lieutenant up and down, appraisingly.

"Good evening, Lieutenant," the faceless man said.

McEwen said nothing but glared at the man with the ember red eyes. The woman next to Gil handed her earrings, rings and broach over to the faceless man who dropped them into the bag. McEwen did not move.

"Now, lieutenant, don't do anything you'll regret later." His tone was mocking.

Gil removed his wallet from his inside jacket pocket, unstrapped his watch and handed them over.

"I'll take the badge as well, lieutenant," the faceless man said. "It's pinned to back of your lapel."

McEwen, despite his seething anger, was noticeably taken aback. No one except for his closest friends knew he carried his badge there. Of course he hadn't needed to wear it. His first year as a detective, he was attacked by a knife wielding man crazy on dope. He lunged at McEwen, bringing the knife down hard at his chest. The tip of the blade broke against the brass of the badge and gave McEwen the life-saving second he needed to elbow the man into unconsciousness. From that day on, he always wore his badge pinned in the very same place, but under his lapel.

Another forty victims and the bag was half full and must have weighed thirty pounds, but the faceless man's goon carried it as if it was stuffed with feathers. When it was Stephen's turn, he purposefully kept his head down. As he handed over his watch, the I.D. bracelet Sue had given him and his wallet, he noticed something. The toes of the faceless man's shoes were beaded with moisture. Not wet from weather, which would have dried by now, but recent droplets. From nowhere, a drop of liquid splashed onto the toe of the faceless man's shoe.

Stephen looked up into the shadow void of the faceless man's face and saw his glowing eyes shimmer as if he were seeing them through a wavering mist.

The faceless man moved on. Methodically making his way down the line. The last two were Sister Mary Catherine and Sue McEwen. The faceless man held out his hand in front of the sister.

"I have nothing," she said.

The faceless man pointed to the gold cross hung around the nun's neck. Instinctively, she clutched it to her breast.

"The cross, Sister," he said.

"I will not," she said defiantly.

The goon moved in closer, towering over the petite nun. The faceless man reached out and Sue, stepping forward, slapped the faceless man's hand away. There was the blur of a fist and the loud crack of flesh against flesh as the goon backhanded Sue, sending her to her knees. Stephen bolted forward. The giant at the center of the room whipped his gun in Stephen's direction, ready to fire. Although just as mad at seeing his daughter struck, Lt. McEwen hurriedly grabbed his protege's shoulder and pulled him back in line.

Sister Mary Catherine unclasped the cross and handed it to the faceless man and then knelt to help Sue to her feet. Her cheek had already begun to swell from the blow as tears of anger filled her eyes.

"I'll take the rest of it," the faceless man said.

"The rest of what," Sue said bitterly.

"The raffle money," he said casually. "It's in a canvas bag just behind the stage. Go and get it and bring it to me. And I'm sure I don't need to tell you what will happen if you do anything imprudent."

Sue did as she was told. In five of the longest minutes of Stephen's life, Sue returned with a canvas bag marked with the event's logo and handed it to the faceless man who, in turn, placed it into the bag containing the stolen goods. The faceless man walked toward the door, with his goons following, backing out with him, guns at the ready. As the sound of the closing door echoed through the hall, it was still several seconds before anyone moved.

Stephen ran to the door, followed closely by Lieutenant McEwen and Police Chief Peter Thatcher, Stephen's father. The door seemed to have been locked from the outside, although the door could only be truly locked from the inside. McEwen got the ax from the fire cabinet and started prying the door open. There was a loud crack as the door broke open followed by a screeching high-pitched whine. Suddenly the doorway filled with a cloud of noxious red smoke.

"Chloroform gas!" Stephen yelled, covering his nose and mouth. Within seconds the police chief and the lieutenant were on their knees, coughing violently. McEwen grabbed the Chief and dragged him away from the door as Stephen, his pocket handkerchief pressed across his nose and mouth, ran blindly into the fog. By the time he made it to the street, his head reeling from the effect of the gas, the faceless man and his cohorts were gone.

The next morning's papers were full of the previous evening's events.

"*Faceless Devil Robs Hope From Dying Children*" the Great City Examiner's headline read.

"*Charity Robbed Blind By Devil Eyes,*" ran the headline of the Great City Times Dispatch.

Ash trays overflowed with cigarette butts. Cold cups of coffee crowded Chief Thatcher's desk and side table. Lt. Gil McEwen and Detective Stephen Thatcher had been meeting with the chief since nine the morning after the brazen robbery. They had been going over witness statements hoping for some insight into the faceless man's identity.

"Mr. George Williams said a man with glowing eyes and two of his trained gorillas robbed him and his wife," Lt. McEwen reported. "Trained *gorillas.*"

"The man had a tail," the Chief read from a report, "that flicked under his cape. I've seen pictures of the devil in the bible. There's no doubt we were robbed by the devil himself."

"Here's a report from a Mrs. Angelia Warren," Stephen began.

"The wife of Professor Arnold Warren," McEwen added. "He's head of the English Literature Department at the University."

"Mrs. Warren reports," Stephen continued, "that the man with no face floated several feet off the ground and that flames shot out of his eyes."

"We've been through how many? Fifty? Sixty reports?" the Chief said, "and we're no closer to getting anything useable than we were last night."

"I'll tell you what I know," Lt. McEwen said, "the Moon Man is tied up in this somehow."

"I don't know, Gil," the Chief said. "This just doesn't sound like him. I'll grant you, he's a sly one and he's not above a little larceny, but robbing from a charity like this? It just seems so out of character."

"Character!" the lieutenant scoffed. "He's an amoral thief! A criminal! Maybe he didn't actually do the crime but he's behind it. I can tell you. Character? He's scum of the lowest kind and I mean to put him behind bars where he belongs."

They were quiet for a long moment. The only sound in the room was the steady tick-tock of the wall clock and the shuffle of papers as the chief started stacking the witness reports into manageable piles.

"Did anyone notice his shoes?" Stephen asked.

"Shoes?" the lieutenant said.

"Yes," Stephen said. "There were drops of moisture on the toes of his shoes."

"So?" McEwen said. "He probably walked through some damp grass or a puddle."

"I made a point not to look into his eyes," Stephen continued. "I didn't want to give him the satisfaction of thinking I cared a lick about him. So I concentrated on his shoes. As he stood in front of me, a couple of drops of moisture landed on the toes of his shoes. I think the faceless effect has something to do with a concentration of mist. I think he wears a device that produces a dense vapor mist that conceals his face and makes it appear as if it's a wavering shadow."

"And that would account for the fresh drops of moisture falling to his shoes," the Chief reasoned.

"The only time he turned," the lieutenant observed, "was right at the door to leave. I didn't think much about it at the time, but it looked as if he were hunched, as if there was something wrong with his back."

"Maybe he had some kind of tank strapped to his back, under his cape that produced the faceless effect," Stephen continued.

"Stephen," the Chief said, "run your theory by Dr. Pendergast. If anyone can make sense of it, he can. Gil, I want you to head back to the ballroom. Have a look around. See if we might have missed anything. We've got to stop this guy before he strikes again.

"Again?" McEwen said. "You think he will?"

"I know he will, Gil," the Chief said. "It's just a matter of time. Time we don't have."

It was after ten when Stephen walked through the front door of his two-story stucco house. The house and surrounding property belonged to his Uncle Seth. It was out in the middle of "nowhere" and no one in the family really wanted anything to do with it after Seth died. And so, by default, Stephen acquired the house and the twenty acres on which it stood. As it turned out, it was the perfect location for the Moon Man's headquarters.

Ned "Angel" Dargan was waiting for Stephen when he came in. The former boxer, whose career was cut short by a brutal beating in the ring, found himself homeless, living in a cardboard box under the Errol James bridge. That's where Stephen found him. Stephen knew Angel's story and decided to give the former pugilist a helping hand. From that day forward,

Angel had become Stephen's devoted friend and compatriot. Angel was one of two people in the world who knew his friend's secret. By day he was Detective Stephen Thatcher. By night, he was the Moon Man a modern-day Robin Hood. When the cops failed to act, to intervene in the cause of social justice, it was the Moon Man who fought for the little guy. Sometimes that fight skirted the law which put him at odds with the very thing he swore to uphold. It was a risky business, but it was a risk he was prepared to take.

"Right is always right," he once told Angel, "even if it goes against the law." It's what he believed and it was the way he lived.

"Any news?" Angel asked, taking Stephen's coat.

"Not really," Stephen said following Angel into the living room. "I ran the mist concentration theory by Dr. Prendergast and he seems to think it has possibilities. He's going to look into it and get back to me."

"And?" Angel asked.

Stephen smiled. How well his friend knew him.

"And I think the Moon Man needs to have a second look at the crime scene. There has got to be a clue we overlooked. McEwen went back to the ballroom and came away with nothing."

"The Lieutenant sees what he wants to see," Angel observed.

"Right now," Stephen said, "all he sees is the hand of the Moon Man in it."

"Of course he does," Angel said dismissively. "I wouldn't be surprised if he tried to blame the sinking of the Titanic on the Moon Man. Or the Hindenburg disaster."

"He's a good man, deep down," Stephen said.

"Would you think that way if he wasn't Sue's father?"

Stephen paused and turned to look at his friend. After a moment of silence, Stephen turned back, heading to the secret staircase that led to the Moon Man's hidden lair.

Down two flights of stairs they came to an iron clad door. To the left of the door was a rectangle about the size of the man's hand. Arranged in the center of the rectangle was a series of numbered buttons. Stephen pressed seven of them in a particular sequence and the door slid aside. The room was large, low-ceilinged, white-walled, brightly lit. It was literally like going from night to day, leaving the stairwell to the Moon Man's sanctuary. The walls were lined with shelves arranged with a mind-boggling collection of gizmos and gadgets. One corner was devoted to machine tooling equipment and a small foundry. Opposite it looked like a laboratory outfitted with the latest in scientific instruments. Shielded against a wall was a firing range. Near the center of the room was a large U-shaped work space set with various lighting systems. Curtained in the far corner was a darkroom. Most notable was the glass door closet with several shelves arranged with the Moon Man's signature mirrored Argus Glass helmets and next to them hung a dozen black capes, each with an attached pair of matching black leather gloves.

As soon as Angel and Stephen crossed the threshold, the door closed automatically behind them. While Angel prepared the Moon Man's helmet and cape, Stephen began the preparation to become his alter ego. He stripped down to his boxers and pulled on a pair of black trousers specially tailored to accommodate several hidden pockets. Then, on with a custom made bullet proof vest. So thin, it took up no more space than an undershirt but could stop a bullet fired at close range. His shoes were outfitted with a special ribbed rubber sole that quelled the sound of footsteps even on the most polished surface and reduced the impact of walking through gravel to little more than a dry rustling.

Angel handed Stephen the holster with his .38 special and helped him secure it. After checking the gun, making sure it was in good, safe working order, he re-holstered it. Putting on the Moon Man's helmet always gave Stephen an odd kind of thrill. Everything viewed from within the helmet took on a heightened illumination. Objects appeared sharper. Instead of sound being dulled and muffled, as would be expected, sound seemed to become amplified. The down side was that audio-direction was all but lost. Something that sounded as if it were right in front of him could easily be behind him or to his side. But over the years, Stephen had learned to make accommodations.

Angel fit the helmet, securing the neck brace and adjusting the ventilation system until Stephen gave him the thumbs-up. On with the cape. On with the gloves and Stephen Thatcher disappeared into the vigilant crime fighter, the Moon Man. Angel gave him a knuckle bump to the helmet, Stephen responded with a thumbs-up and they exited through another iron door at the back of the room.

The elevator took them to a small subterranean garage. Two identical cars were parked and ready. The men had worked over the course of months to strip out any identifying elements to the automobiles. It was neither a Buick or a Ford. A Cadillac or a Packard, but was in fact, all of them. More than once, the police had been thrown off their track by a confounding lack of a reliable description regarding the Moon Man's get-away vehicle.

"The alley next to the Ballroom?" Angel asked.

Stephen gave him the thumbs-up and they were off, up through the ascending tunnel, through to the well-concealed exit that emptied onto the side road a half a mile from Stephen's home. A light rain had begun to fall. A half moon dissected by skittering clouds turned the landscape into a kind of underwater tableau.

Angel parked behind the Ballroom, next to a low brick wall. He got out grabbing the rope ladder from the backseat and hooked it over the top of the wall. He held it steady as the Moon Man climbed up and over. During the day, when Stephen and the Lieutenant examined the crime scene, Stephen felt they'd missed something in the alley. Debris had been cleared through its center, a space big enough to accommodate a parked car. Did the Lieutenant notice the same thing? Stephen didn't think so and he wasn't going to mention it. The only way to pull the focus away from the Moon Man was to solve the mystery of the Faceless Man. With Gil McEwen's single-mined obsession with the Moon Man, any clue would have to point to the Moon Man's guilt. On the other side of the brick wall, the Moon Man stood motionless and let the scene reveal itself to him. This he did at every crime scene. It was as if he were opening himself up to its secrets. Every crime scene has something to say, and Stephen felt that by keeping an open mind, without preconceptions, he was more likely to hear what it wanted to tell him.

There it was, a tire track impressed into a small patch of sand. As he examined it, he noticed a trail of discoloration leading from where the backdoor of a parked car might have been. Red stained the loose collection of rumpled paper and empty bottles. A residue from the smoke bombs the Faceless Man used at his escape.

"Don't you dare move," the Moon Man heard a short distance away. He knew that voice only too well. He looked up to see the shadowed figure of Lt. Gil McEwen standing resolute, his gun drawn and aimed at the Moon Man's chest.

"I knew I'd find you here," the lieutenant said. "I knew you were mixed up in this mess. I've been waiting a long time to put you behind bars, Moon Man, and tonight that is going to happen."

The Moon Man took a step back toward the rope ladder. McEwen stepped forward and raised his gun. The first shot went wide sending

The Moon Man let the scene reveal itself to him.

bits of exploded brick into the Moon Man's back. Just as the Moon Man reached the rope ladder, McEwen shot again. The bullet cut through the rope attached to the support hook. The Moon Man's weight on the rope rung completed the break sending him to his knees.

McEwen approached cautiously, gun at the ready. The Moon Man got to his feet, his back pressed tight against the wall. His options were as narrow as they could be. Be caught by the father of his girlfriend, arrested and suffer the shame and humiliation that would spread out like pool of poison, or shoot and wound the lieutenant and make his escape.

The Moon Man watched the lieutenant withdraw a pair of handcuffs for his pocket and flip open a cuff. He advanced slowly as if he expected the Moon man to leap at him like a cornered tiger.

"Put your hands up!" McEwen ordered.

The Moon Man did as he was told. Suddenly, he felt strong hands grip his wrists, and within seconds he was hoisted over the wall as if he weighed no more than a bag of flour. McEwen fired three shots, the last ripped through the cuff of the Moon Man's trousers. Angel carried the Moon Man to the car and deposited him in the front seat as if he were a sleepy toddler on his way home from grandma's house. As they sped away they could hear the lieutenant cursing a blue streak that would have made a sailor blush.

"I'm so excited," Sue said to her friend Olivia. They were in a taxi on their way to the Great City Metropolitan Museum of Art. "Just think, we'll be seeing some of the real treasures from King Louis XIV's court."

"My mom saw it yesterday and she said it was to die for!" Olivia said "There's the Chalice of the Sun. Solid gold covered in diamonds and rubies with the king's sun emblem sculpted into the handle."

"I know," Sue said. "I can't wait!"

The taxi pulled up in front of the museum. A line of anxious attendees snaked out the main entrance and down the stairs to the sidewalk.

"Stephen got me advance tickets," Sue said as she and her friend walked to the bronze double doors.

"He's such a dear. You are so lucky."

"Don't I know it!"

The two friends entered the museum, had their tickets punched, bought the official deluxe program and followed the signs to the main gallery. On their way they bumped into several people they knew and heard glowing reviews of the exhibit they were about to see. The Museum had never hosted an exhibition this prestigious and they both felt as if they were about to witness a little history in the making.

As they approached the main gallery in which the exhibition was being held, they were confronted with a line of people forty deep and three and four across.

"What's all this?" Sue asked a white-haired gentlemen at the end of the line.

"They're only letting in twenty people at a time," he said. "Guess they're worried about security or something."

Sue thanked the older man as she and Olivia exchanged exasperated looks. As they waited, they made small talk with some of the people in line. The white-haired gent was named Orville Ashenbach. He and he wife, who succumbed to lung cancer the year before, had been in Paris for their twentieth anniversary and had visited Versailles. From that visit onward the Ashenbachs had been avid amateur scholars of the Sun King.

"He was inordinately proud of his legs," Orville told them. "You almost can't find a portrait of him that he doesn't show them off. They have a very good copy of the Rigaud portrait of him showing off his royal gams. It's oddly endearing I think."

They inched their way forward until they were next in line to enter the gallery. Olivia looked behind her to see a line the stretched out around the corner.

"Guess we got here just in time," she said, as the doors opened and she and Sue and eighteen other people were guided into the gallery.

The Grand Gallery was situated in the center of the museum. It was a large round room with a domed ceiling which provided an abundance of natural light. In the center of the room was a glass case thirty feet across and ten feet tall that housed the precious relics of the Sun King. The room echoed with stunned gasps as the visitors were struck, almost as one, with the splendor of what was before them.

"There's the chalice," Olivia pointed out.

The two friends slowly made their way to the chalice and stood before it in wonder. It was eighteen inches tall and so richly carved and decorated it would take several hours to fully appreciate its beauty.

Orville had shuffled up next to them. "It was said that Louis would bath his favorite Papillion puppies in it," he said pointing to the chalice.

"Look at the size of those diamonds," Sue observed. "I didn't know diamonds could be that big."

Olivia held out her hand as if she were admiring a ring on her finger. "I think that one," she said, pointing to a large, slightly yellow stone set into a golden cherub's hands, "would make a lovely wedding ring. Don't you think?"

The ladies laughed as they moved on to view the rest of the treasures. Sue saw a couple of the guards move from door to door, key locking each one. There was some commotion coming from behind the door at the far end of the gallery. As she turned to it, the doors burst open. Two giants entered holding machine guns. They were dressed in peculiarly tailored black suits, wearing odd wide-brimmed hats. They were followed by the Faceless Man. The doors were quickly locked behind them by a museum guard.

Sue reached for Olivia's hand and held it tight. "Stay calm," she whispered.

The Faceless Man seemed to float just above the marble floor. "Please everyone," he said in his slightly accented voice, "there's no need for anyone to be hurt. If you'd all line up against the wall," pointing to the wall on which hung the portrait of Louis XIV, "everything will be fine."

Sue made sure to try and keep her head turned away from the Faceless Man. As the visitors took their places against the wall, one of the giants used his elbow to smash the glass out of the cases. The sound was frightening as sheets of glass shattered against the polished marble floor. He withdrew a large black cloth bag from his coat pocket and systematically began removing artifacts from their pedestals. One by one, the priceless gemstone and gold pieces were placed in the bag with surprising delicacy, considering the size and brutal appearance of the thief.

After a few minutes it was clear he was interested in certain pieces, leaving some untouched. The Faceless Man looked on, his eyes blazing ember bright in his fathomless shadowed face. Olivia began to weep softly. Sue tried to calm her friend which seemed to make her even more unsettled.

The Faceless Man moved toward them. Sue kept her head down, trying to keep her face from view.

"It will be over soon," he said to Olivia. "Over soon."

Olivia turned and buried her face in her hands, pressing close to Sue. The move made Sue raise her head. The Faceless Man, recognizing Sue, laughed.

"We meet again!" he said, a dark delight in his voice.

She straightened her shoulders back in defiance and looked clear eyed and unafraid into the Faceless Man's undulating void.

"You won't get away with it," she said firmly.

"But I already have," he said in a kind of sing-song tone.

The goon with the bag signaled he'd finished his job and stepped back from the case, shouldering the nearly full bag and raising his machine gun, swaying it back and forth, alert to the slightest threat.

The Faceless Man raised his hand and the giant standing behind him bent down. The Faceless Man whispered something to him and the giant stood. It would be wrong to call the expression that lifted the corners of his liver-lipped mouth a smile. But there was a malicious glee in it that almost reached his eyes. He shouldered his gun, took a step forward, and pulled Sue away from Olivia in a move so quick; the girl stumbled against the wall and slid to the floor. Olivia screamed as did a woman somewhere down the line. Sue was silent in her defiance.

She tried to pull away but the giant held her tight, his huge hands gripped tight to her shoulders. The bag man backed toward the door, gun at the ready. He was joined by this fellow monster-of-a-man, and their Lord of Evil. A guard quickly unlocked the door. Just as they were to exit, there was a loud thud followed by a high-pitched hissing sound. Within seconds the room began to fill with a dense red smoke. The sounds of the doors being locked as the criminals left were drowned out by a cacophony of writhing coughs and desperate cries of fear and panic. One by one, the visitors collapsed into chloroform-induced unconsciousness.

Sue woke in absolute darkness. She actually held her hand up in front of her face and saw nothing but the impenetrable black that surrounded her.

"Miss McEwen," a slightly accented voice said.

It sounded as if it came from across the room and yet so nearby she swatted at the space around her as if to ward off an annoying insect. Two slits of red appeared, floating in the dark some distance from her. Instantly, they became wide blazing eyes of flame.

"Sue Ellen McEwen," the Faceless Man said. "Twenty-two years old. Five foot seven, one-hundred and twenty-nine pounds, brown hair and eyes. A heart-shaped birthmark on your back near your left shoulder. Your father is Lieutenant Gilbert McEwen of the Great City police department. For the past three years you have been dating police Detective Stephen Thatcher, son of Chief of Police Peter Thatcher. Have I left anything out?"

"Go to hell," Sue said angrily.

"Oh, and," he continued, "you seem to have, more than once, encountered the Moon Man. In fact, there have been several occasions when he has come to your rescue. Has he not?"

Sue said nothing. As she stared at the two burning ovals of the Faceless Man's eyes, they seemed to undulate in waves of motion. Although they didn't move, the sound of his voice came closer. She thought she could feel the heat of him so nearby, she could reach out and touch him.

"I know the truth about your friend," the Faceless Man said.

Sue's heart clutched in panic at the thought that this villain knew the Moon Man's secret.

"He's not the menace he's made out to be," he continued. "In fact, he's something of a do-gooder. Stealing from the rich and corrupt to support and nourish the poor. Kind of like a modern day Roger Hood."

"*Robin* Hood, you idiot," Sue corrected.

"Yes, of course, *Robin* Hood," he said. "I have no worries about the police finding me. They could not find the seat of their pants with both hands. But the Moon Man, he is a worry. If anyone can disrupt my plans, it will, I believe, be him."

"And when he does, you and your goons will go to prison for the rest of your unnatural lives!" Sue said, righteousness ascending in her voice.

He was silent for as long moment, his eyes glowing malevolently from across the room. And in that silence, she understood. And that understanding ran a cold desperation down her spine.

"Yes," he said as if reading her thoughts. "He will, of course, come to your rescue. And when he does, I'll be there."

She meant to say something. Something flip. Something clever. Something to show this faceless evil his threats were a hollow farce. But she couldn't for the fear and worry choking her.

She heard a small popping sound and a high-pitched hiss. A pungent sweetness engulfed her as she faded from consciousness.

Moments later, a dim light gave definition to the small room. A door opened and one of the giants entered, picked Sue up from the daybed as if she were no larger than a rag doll and carried her from the room, with the Faceless Man close behind.

"Is everything ready?" the Faceless Man asked.

The giant grunted.

"Good," the Faceless Man said. "By this time tomorrow, I'll have destroyed the Moon Man and Great City will be mine." He chuckled to himself. "And to think, I'll have the unwitting help of Lieutenant McEwen to accomplish it."

The giant grunted again.

"The girl?" the Faceless Man said in answer to his goon's question. "I don't think it's likely she'll survive. She may. But I doubt it. It's little concern of mine. The king does not worry over the fate of a pawn."

"Please, Olivia, you'll need to calm down if we're going to save Sue," Stephen said as gently as he could, trying to keep the anxious tension out of his voice.

Olivia was hysterical when Stephen found her curled into a ball on the floor of the main gallery. He managed to get her to her feet and guided her to the museum director's office. Stephen could not help but feel the desperation of time slipping by as he watched the sweep of the second hand of the wall clock over Olivia's shoulder.

"He grabbed her by the shoulders," Olivia managed to say between ragged breaths. "The look in her eyes. She wasn't afraid. She was angry. She was so brave. Oh, Stephen, what's going to happen to her?"

He knelt in front of her and put his hand on her quivering shoulder. "Is there anything else, Olivia," Stephen said calmly. "Anything at all."

The girl sat up, her cheeks streaked with tears. She looked out into the distance as if trying to pull in a shifting image. "His gloves," Olivia said.

"Whose gloves?" Stephen asked.

"The man without a face," Olivia replied. "They're custom made. A little place on Basil Avenue. My dad used to have his gloves special made because of his arthritis."

Stephen slid back into his chair opposite the girl and leaned in, taking in every word. "How do you know?"

"The man's name is Arthur Stanslensy," Olivia said. "He sews his initials into the back of each glove. It's kind of a like a curlicue. My dad thought it looked a little *feminine* and asked him not to put it on his gloves but he refused. So, my dad started having his gloves made somewhere else."

Stephen sat back and looked at Sue's friend intently.

"What?" she said, feeling uncomfortable under his gaze.

"I think you just saved Sue's life, Olivia."

At the mention of her friend's name, tears began to flow. She tried to speak but the words wouldn't come. Stephen stood, guided Olivia to her feet and gave her a comforting hug.

Morris Winebottom was a smart as a whip and dedicated as they come. He'd graduated from the academy at the ripe old age of twenty, with honors. He'd been at the Great City Police department for a little over six months, three of those working with Stephen as a junior detective. Morris walked into Stephen's office holding a folded piece of paper and handed it to his partner.

"What's this?" Stephen asked.

"The low-down on Arthur Stanslensy," Morris said, settling into the chair opposite Stephen's desk. "He immigrated to this country twenty years ago from Russia. Never married. Lives with his sister who works at the shop with him. Arthur is sixty-six years old. His sister, Marta, is thirty-two."

Stephen raised an eyebrow.

"He's something of a celebrity among glove aficionados," Morris continued. "Something to do with the leather or something. Get this. A pair of his custom made gloves goes for fifty bucks!"

Stephen whistled. "Fifty bucks. Holy cow!"

"I know," Morris said. "There's a waiting list too. You put an order in for a pair of gloves in the summer, you're lucky to get them by next spring. That's why most people who buy from him buy a couple of pairs at a time."

"Does he keep sales records?"

"Does he keep sales records!?" Morris said. "The guy probably has a record of what he had for lunch on Monday, October 15, 1888. And what he tipped. The guy keeps records."

Stephen opened the folded and paper. There were two columns of tightly crammed scribbles.

"What's all this?"

"A list of sales of custom made men's gloves for the past five years," Morris said.

Stephen's look of exasperation was so painfully obvious it made Morris smile. The junior detective reached into his inside coat pocket, removed another folded paper and handed it across Stephen's desk.

"It's a list of gloves sales for the last year. Size 7.5 to 8.5. Average. The description of the Faceless Man put him at about five foot nine. That puts him smack dab in the middle of average."

Stephen opened the new page. There were eight names with addresses.

"The guys with the red marks by their names are out of the country and have been during the Faceless Man's events."

"So, that leaves us with six potential suspects."

"Right." Morris concurred. From his coat pocket he removed two business cards and handed them to Stephen.

"Reginald Draper, Modern Men's Style magazine?" Stephen said, reading one of the cards. "Jerome Gayle, Modern Men's Style magazine," reading the other.

"I figure we go in as cops, we get nothing," Morris said, nodding to the cards in Stephen's hand. "But we go in as magazine writers doing a story on the best custom glove makers in the city and their discriminating clientele…"

"Morris," Stephen said. "If you're not chief in ten years then there is no God in heaven."

Morris smiled as the tips of his ears flushed red.

James Arden lived on the twelfth floor of the Windsor Arms apartments in the posh neighborhood of Excelsior Commons. He was an elderly gentleman who wore thick lensed glasses and a toupee that might have once matched his hair color. Yes, he bought his gloves at Stanslensy's. Had done for years. Stephen and Morris thanked him and checked him off the suspect list.

Armand DeGrasse had unusually long fingers. When held up to Morris's they were a good three-quarters of an inch beyond the junior detective's fingertips, yet Mr. De Grasse's and Morris's palms were nearly the same size. He purchase three pairs of gloves from Arthur and was very pleased with his purchases. Although he did wish the AS stitched in the back of each glove was a little less prominent. He was marked off the list.

It took Theo Ballentine ten minutes to come to the door after it was answered by a *personal assistant*. When he did arrive in a smoking jacket and carrying a book cradled in his arm, he was clearly annoyed at having been interrupted. He was between 5'9" and 5'11", of average build and spoke with a slight accent. French Swiss as it was later revealed. His gaze was intense and disdainful. Yes, he owned several pairs of the custom made gloves. Why wouldn't he? Several minutes into a difficult conversation, Morris noticed something change in Theo's demeanor. A heightened awareness, as if he recognized Stephen. He became less belligerent and almost… almost, friendly. They thanked him for his time.

"You saw it too?" Morris asked when they were back in the car on their way to the next name on the list.

"Yes," Stephen said. "But it might mean nothing. My face was all over the place after the Houghton case."

"Maybe," Morris said. "But let's see what we can find out about our Mr. Fancy Pants."

Donald Millerson was drunk. It was 3:30 in the afternoon. He lived in a beautiful old two-story brick house set in a picture perfect landscaped yard of several acres. When the two men introduced themselves as writers for Modern Men's Style magazine, Mr. Millerson invited them in. The living room was large and well appointed. A carved granite fireplace took up most of the north facing wall. To the east, a bank of floor to ceiling windows flooded the room with late afternoon light. The entire room might have been lifted from an English detective movie, replete with a pair of yorkies that followed their inebriated master as if he were going to dispense bites of filet mignon at any moment.

"Please, sit," Millerson said pointing to a couch set across from a pair of high-backed easy chairs. "Can I get you gentlemen something to drink?"

Stephen and Morris declined. Millerson topped off his snifter with a healthy pour from a cut crystal decanter and sat unsteadily in a chair opposite the couch.

"I've been buying my gloves from Arthur for years," Millerson said. "He's an odd little fellow but a brilliant craftsman."

Both Stephen and Morris sized up their host as the conversation went on. He was the right height and weight and seemed to be in relatively good physical shape, but it was impossible to envision this man doing much else but attending to his dogs and cognac.

"Terrible, that, about the museum," Millerson said. "Terrible. I had tickets to see the exhibition of the Louis's stuff this coming weekend. My father was ambassador to France, back in the day. 'If ever you get the chance, Donnie,' he used to say to me: 'go to Versailles. See how a true king lived.' Seeing Louis's treasures was as close as I was going to get. I'm afraid my traveling days are over. I have a deadly fear of flying and the idea of being on a boat for weeks on end makes me nauseous just thinking about it."

Both Morris and Stephen agreed the theft was a terrible thing.

"I hope that girl is going to be okay," Millerson added.

Morris was about to say something but Stephen tapped the junior detective's shoe with his own.

"Is there a chance we might have a look at a pair of Arthur's gloves?" Stephen asked. "We've seen several pairs so far as part of our research and have noticed the initials Mr. Stanslensy sews into the back of each glove varies a little."

"Let's see what we can find out about our Mr. Fancy Pants."

"You're so right," Millerson said. "They do. I have a pair from five years ago and the initials are almost half the size they are now. It might be Arthur's a little more prideful these days than when he started out. Odd little fellow but what a craftsman!"

If silence could have hung any heavier it would have needed a forklift to move it aside.

"Well, I guess we should be going," Morris said at last.

"Thank you for your time," Stephen said. "We very much appreciate it."

"When did you say the article would be coming out?" Millerson asked.

"Issue after next," Morris said. "That will be up to our editor."

Millerson made to get up from his chair but seemed to have difficulty doing it.

"We'll show ourselves out, if that's okay," Stephen said.

Millerson said that would be fine. They shook hands and headed to the door, the yorkies at their heels hoping for treats. After closing the door behind them, being careful not to crimp a dog in the jamb, and heading down the walkway, Stephen looked over his shoulder at the house. To the left of the front door was a bank of curtained windows. The curtains parted a little near the top of the window, some seven feet above the sill, as if someone were watching them leave.

"There was nothing about Sue's abduction in the papers," Morris said, when they were back in the car.

"That curtain still parted?" Stephen asked.

"Curtain?"

"You know what I think?"

"The whole thing was an act," the rookie said.

"Great minds," Stephen smiled. "You notice how he side stepped us having a look at his gloves? And that thing about the initials being different? I made that up."

"Well, he didn't want us seeing his gloves, that's for sure."

"And you're right," Stephen continued. "No one outside of the investigation knows about Sue being kidnapped. No one."

"So, was he really that drunk that he let it slip," Morris conjectured, "or did he let it slip to draw us in?"

"I'm going to drop you off at the station. Find out everything you can about Donald Millerson. I'll go check out the last two names on the list on my own."

"What about the curtain?' Morris asked.

Stephen told him.

"That would be about eye level for one of the Faceless Man's goons," Morris said.

"That's what I was thinking," Stephen agreed.

Stephen dropped Morris off at headquarters and headed to 256 Bethany Road. A row of parked cars lined both sides of the street. A hearse was parked in the driveway. Samuel Chen passed away four days previously he was told. Sam was checked off the list.

Dusk was beginning to nestle into the top branches of the trees as Stephen pulled up to Corbin House. Stephen hadn't put the address with the name of the house until he saw it. The three towers nearly silhouetted against the waning evening light had been splashed across the front page of the papers for weeks after Great City's most notorious murders. As he got out of the car, he reflexively patted the .45 automatic holstered under his jacket. He hadn't walked a dozen feet when he heard the crack of gunfire. He turned and ran to take cover behind his car as another shot sent a slug into the passenger's side door.

"Police!" Stephen yelled.

He was answered with another blast of gunfire that tore into the sidewalk sending chunks of concrete into the air.

Stephen waited, anticipating another volley of shots that didn't come. He eased around the back of the car, in a running crouch, made it to a large oak near a hedge row. Hidden by the hedge, he ran up to the side of the house, paused, listening. Silence. Through a gap in the hedge he was in the backyard. What had once been an elegant arrangement of walkways, a pond and ornamental shrubs had been left unattended and succumbed to nature's vengeance against order. It took him valuable moments to pick his way through the overgrowth to the backdoor. Again, listening attentively for any warning sounds, hearing nothing, he tried the door.

"Please, Mr. Corbin, put down the gun," Stephen called out.

The old man sat in a chair near the front window, a pistol in his hand. He was startled at the sound of a stranger's voice and raised the gun but without intent.

"It's Stephen Thatcher, Mr. Corbin."

"Stephen?" the old man said, hard times pressing down on each syllable.

"Yes sir," Stephen said. "Please put down the gun. I think we need to have a talk. Would that be okay?"

The old man laid the gun in his lap as Stephen entered the room. A small lamp on the mantle gave faint light to the room ravished by time and neglect. The debris of years accumulated in piles on the floor. Boxes stacked on boxes. Books in random stacks teetered at odd angles. This was a room not lived in. It was a room in which time was waited out until the inevitable end.

"You were the only one who believed me, Stephen," the old man said.

"Yes, sir," Stephen said removing a box from a nearby chair to sit. "I just knew you didn't do it and just had to find the proof, is all."

"If it weren't for you, they'd have hung me for a crime I did not do. You saved my life, young man, such as it is. How have you been, Stephen?"

"I'm a detective now, Mr. Corbin," Stephen said. "I'm working a case and came by to talk with you about some gloves you had made. Arthur Stanslensy?"

"Gloves?"

"Yes, sir," Stephen said. "Custom made gloves."

The old man laughed bitterly. "The trial took everything I had. Everything. I can't afford a pair of gloves from Woolworths, let alone ones custom made."

Stephen was a rookie policeman when the murders at Corbin House were discovered. Jasper Corbin's young wife and her sister had been brutally murdered. Both had been raped and their bodies savagely mutilated. *Whore* had been written on the wall with the women's blood. Jasper had discovered the bodies, as he told police. He was charged and arrested for the double homicide. That's when the rumors began to fly fast and furious. *The Love Triangle That Turned Deadly!* One of the tabloids ran the story detailing the sordid sexual escapades of the three that often involved others in an immoral orgy of wanton sexual depravity.

Looking at the evidence, Stephen was convinced that Jasper was innocent. He worked the case on his own time, interviewed dozens of people the department hadn't even bothered to contact. Corbin was convicted and sentenced to death. Three days before his execution, Stephen uncovered a critical piece of evidence that led to Jasper's conviction being over turned and to the arrest of his younger brother, William. The trial ruined Jasper financially and emotionally. The last Stephen heard, Jasper had moved to a small apartment on the outskirts of the city, alone, broken and destitute.

"I had to come back," Jasper explained. "I had no place else to go. I've tried to sell the place over the years, but no one wants to buy a house so tainted by blood."

As evening descended, Stephen listened to Jasper's heartbreaking story and vowed to himself, when the case of the Faceless Man had been solved he'd do whatever he could to help this old man live out the rest of his years in peace and comfort.

"The glove maker, a man by the name of Arthur Stanslensy, kept meticulous records of all his sales to men with a glove size of 7.5 to 8.5 over the past year. And he has you listed as having purchased three pairs four months ago."

Jasper held up his hands. The fingers of both were gnarled into near fists, knuckles swollen into knobs of a worsted flesh.

"I don't understand," Stephen said as much to himself as he did to Jasper.

"Detective, eh?" Jasper said. "I'd say its time for a little detecting, Stephen."

Stephen sat in silence, listening to the chorus frogs sing in the swampy pond. "Can I have a look at your mail?" Stephen asked at last.

Jasper pointed a crooked finger to a pile on the floor by the front door. There were months of unopened correspondence. Stephen brought a stack of it near the mantle light and began sorting through it.

An envelope marked *A.S.Custom Gloves. 13308 S Manhattan Place, Great City* was half way through the pile, unopened. Stephen opened it and removed the folded paper. The letterhead was an embossed version of Stanslensy's signature initials sewn into each of his custom made gloves. The letter read.

Dear Mr. Corbin,

Thank you for purchasing three pairs of my Worthington Style gloves. I must admit, they were quite a challenge for me to create, but a welcome one, I can assure you. I do, of course understand your desire to have your gloved hands appear whole and unaffected. The stigma of the loss of a finger I can only imagine. Creating a left hand gloved with an articulated little finger tested all my skill. I hope, most sincerely, that you are as pleased with the result as am I. Thank you again for trusting me with such a delicate matter. I've enclosed a copy of your receipt as you left the original at my shop by accident.

Signed, A. Stanslensy, glover.

"Missing little finger," Stephen said absently.

"Missing finger?" Jasper asked.

"Well," Stephen said. "It appears the little finger on your left hand is missing, according to Mr. Stanslensy."

"Not me," Jasper said. "My nephew, Anton."

"What have you got?" Stephen asked Morris. It was three o'clock in the morning and both men had been up all night trying to get what they could on Anton Corbin.

"Anton Corbin," Morris read from a hastily complied report, "is thirty-two years old. Five feet nine inches tall, one hundred and sixty three pounds. He was born in this country but was taken to Argentina by his mother at the age of nine. There was an indictment of arrest for him in Argentina for running a criminal organization known as the *Four and Five*. He was twenty years old. Members of the gang were required to have the little fingers of their left hands cut off as a show of loyalty. He fled the country and vanished into thin air. There's no record of him reentering the U.S. What else did Jasper have to say?"

"He said the boy was too smart for his own good," Stephen said. "Jasper said he was always a little odd. He was a nasty little boy and cruel. He was implicated in the drowning death of a neighbor boy. He was eight or nine, as Jasper remembers."

"That would coincide with him being taken out of the country," Morris said.

"Exactly," Stephen agreed. "He did say that the trial had a big impact on the boy. Anton's mother and Jasper corresponded throughout the trial and afterward. And sometime later, cashier's cheques started showing up anonymously. They were sent from New York but were drawn from a bank in Buenos Aries."

"Anton?" Morris asked.

"Jasper thought so."

Stephen closed his eyes, titling his head to rest it on the chair back.

After a long moment, Morris asked, "How you holding up?"

"I'm worried sick about Sue," Stephen said without opening his eyes. "I feel helpless. I don't know what to do. I can't stop thinking the worst but I can't let myself. I can't give in to despair."

"We'll find her, boss."

"I hope to God we do, Morris," Stephen said. "I hope to God we do before it's too late."

"Well, I guess the lieutenant is wrong about the Moon Man being involved," Morris said, changing the subject.

"He'll never admit it," Stephen said, looking at the junior detective. "Anything and everything that happens in this city is tied to the Moon Man, as far as Gil is concerned. But I can't worry about that now."

Stephen straightened papers on his desk into piles of relevance while Morris went to the donut shop across the street for a couple of cups of fresh coffee and some day-old pastries. Ten minutes later, Stephen's door burst open. Morris stood, clutching a paper bag and cup of coffee in one hand and second cup of java and a single sheet of paper in the other; a look of dread distorting his handsome face.

"What?" Stephen asked in alarm.

Morris strode to Stephen's desk and awkwardly handed him the piece of paper. As Stephen read, the color drained from his face.

"When did this come in?" he asked rereading the sheet that shook in his trembling hands.

"Just now," Morris said. "Dropped off at the front desk. No, they didn't see who it was"

"Anybody see it?"

"You mean does anyone else know what it says?"

"Yes."

"No one has read this but me and you," Morris said. "It came in a sealed envelope addressed to Detectives Thatcher and Winebottom."

"I'm not sure what to make of it," Stephen said, forcing himself to consider the note as a detective and not as the boyfriend of his kidnapped lover.

Sue McEwen is safe. For now. For her to remain so, the Moon Man must come to the observation platform of the Liberty Tower at Midnight, tonight. If the police become involved, she will be killed. Specifically, if Lieutenant McEwen makes a appearance, she will be killed. The Moon Man alone can save Miss McEwen. If her life means anything to you, you will follow my instructions precisely. Signed, The Faceless Terror.

Morris sat in the chair as if the wind had just been knocked out of him. "What are we going to do?" he asked.

"What can we do?" Stephen said. "The problem is, how do we get word to the Moon Man?"

There was a sealed envelope sitting at the center of Lieutenant Gil McEwen's desk when he arrived at the station a little after seven-thirty in the morning. He set his briefcase down, took a long sip of his first of what would be many cups of coffee and considered the envelope. His name was written in an elegant hand across its center in blue ink. The *G* in Gilbert had a long, drop down flourish that reminded him of his mother's handwriting. He reached into the top drawer of his desk, removed the letter opener that looked like a miniature dagger and sliced it open.

Angry tears filled his eyes as he read. What should he do? His first instinct was to assemble the team, review their options and then put the plan into action. But that course of action would only get his daughter killed. He knew the Moon Man was behind the robberies, and now he had proof. To learn that Sue had been abducted by that bastard caught him by surprise. Even he had to admit that the Moon Man, more than once, had come to his daughter's aid. Wasn't it the Moon Man who risked his own life to board that speeding train, carry Sue to safety moments before it jumped the tracks and plummeted into the Bachen River? When Sue unwittingly walked into a robbery in progress at the Great City Nation's Trust, wasn't it the Moon Man, who put himself between his daughter and the gunman taking the bullet meant for her? Unless the Lieutenant came to the observation platform of the Liberty Tower building at half-past midnight, the Moon Man threatened to throw her off, bound and gagged, to her death seventy stories below.

"Tell no one," the note read. "And come alone. Signed, The Moon Man."

Angel was not fond of heights. For a man whose fear tolerance was off the charts, a step ladder made him break out into a cold sweat. He stood outside of the Liberty Tower entrance trying to talk himself into entering the lobby. A traffic cop across the street gave him suspicious looks as Angel walked up and back muttering to himself.

"It's only the lobby," he said. "Only the lobby. That's ground floor. Lobby Lobby. Lobby."

He pushed through the revolving doors into the vast, high-ceilinged lobby and took a deep breath. The bank of elevators seemed to mock him. A mother and her young child stood next to an elevator door, the boy hopping with excitement when his mother let him push the UP button. The boy turned to look at Angel and smiled. Was the kid mocking him too? He walked near an elevator and watched the arrow count down the floors. It held at three and then descended to two and one. The doors opened. A group of people got out. They looked fine. Normal. Nobody looked the worse for wear. Some were smiling. Others carried on conversations that must have started on their descent.

He was Angel Dargan, dammit! He'd been in the ring with some of the most brutal, knuckle busting boxers in the business. He never backed down. He never entered the ring scared. Even when he squared off with Mahoney the Mangler. The fight before Angel's, the Mangler broke a guy's neck with a roundhouse to the jaw. If Angel could get into the ring with the Mangler, he could get into an elevator and ride to the observation platform, seventy stories up, and check the place out for the Moon Man.

It took him three tries before he could muster the courage to get into the elevator and ride it to the tenth floor. Another couple to take him to the fortieth floor. He got out at the fiftieth floor and wished to God he had a drink. A good shot of whiskey would have easily bolstered his courage along about then. He figured, by the way his guts were rolling, he'd need many more than a couple of shots.

Angel closed his eyes, took a deep breath walked to the observation platform elevator and pushed the up button.

"You getting out, buddy?" a man said to him when the elevator stopped moving.

Angel had heard about the roof top garden. He'd seen pictures of it in Great City Quarterly magazine. But seeing it in person took his breath away. It was a fantasyland of geometric trimmed shrubs, large flowering pots over flowing with blossoms of every color of the rainbow, vine-covered trellises and topiaries sculpted into a menagerie of circus animals. He followed the brick-lined path to a small pond replete with a fountain, a waterfall and goldfish the size of small dogs swimming leisurely back and forth under the misting spray. Following the path farther, the hedge that cloistered the garden opened up to a view of the city that made him forget his fear of heights. Almost made him forget why he was there.

Seventy floors up he could see the sunlight turn the Great River, for which the city was named, into a band of gold as it snaked through the eastern edge of the city. There was City Hall. To the north, Great City Pavalion and the ballroom where the Faceless Man struck first. He was so engrossed in the panorama that he almost forgot he was seven hundred feet above the street level below. As beautiful as it was, he saw it for what it would be come midnight; a death trap. True, there was only one way up to the garden and one way down but it was so full of potential traps and ambush spots there would be no way to prepare against a set up.

He walked the entire garden several times, making notes of particularly dangerous sections. In the far southern corner, a hedge enclosed the air conditioning system, and the maintenance shed. Opposite, in the north corner, a section had been closed off that was most likely used for potting and caring for plants, with a watering station and the pump system for the

He walked the entire garden several times.

pond. Stephen and he had eight hours to put together a plan. He was so engrossed in worry, that he barely noticed the elevator ride down. In the lobby, he walked right past Lieutenant McEwen without a second glance.

"It's a set up," Angel told Stephen after giving him a full report on the observation platform and garden. "He'll be able to pick you off as soon as you get off the elevator."

"We're going to have to get the Moon Man ready on site," Stephen said. "We can't run the risk of someone spotting the Moon Man on his way up and alert the police."

"Especially at midnight," Angel said. "You have to transfer to the roof top elevator at the fiftieth floor. Maybe we can find an office someplace we can use."

"Jake Stanley has an office on the fiftieth floor," Stephen remembered.

"The writer?"

"Yep," Stephen said. "He and I go way back, I'm sure he wouldn't mind if we borrowed his place for a little while."

"What he don't know won't hurt him?" Angel chuckled.

"Exactly. I have a key from when he was having all that trouble with the Sokasists Gang. You set everything up?"

"Ready to go, Boss."

"Okay, let's go over it again."

Angel went to the map of the roof top layout they'd gotten from the building manager earlier in the day. Angel pointed to a spot near the fish pond.

"Right will take me back to the elevator," Stephen repeated what he'd learned. "Left will take me to the north corner. Behind the waterfall is canister number two."

"Right. Good."

"I've upgraded the filters in the helmet," Stephen said. "If he's planning on using the gas, it won't have any effect."

"What about ours?"

"Same. Anything other than cyanide and we're fine."

"I don't like you going on your own, Steve. It's too dangerous. You know he'll have his goons with him."

"I can't risk Sue's life because mine might be at stake," Stephen said somberly. "She means the world to me, Angel. I couldn't live with myself if anything happened to her."

They were silent, each lost in thought.

"Okay," Angel pointed to a spot in the map where the hedge opened up to the view of the city.

"At the base of the north opening is canister number three."

Lieutenant McEwen was parked down the block from the Liberty Tower building at 11:00 p.m. It was a surprisingly clear evening considering it had threatened rain through most of the day. His .45 was checked and loaded sitting on the seat next to him, a pair of binoculars rested in the curve of the steering wheel.

At 11:15 p.m. Gill watched a man in a long dark overcoat turn the corner, walking quickly toward the Liberty Tower entrance. There was something familiar about the man's gait but Gil couldn't place it. There was nothing particularly unusual about someone entering the building at such an hour. Several well-known writers along with a couple of artists had offices there and kept unorthodox schedules.

Stephen ever watchful for a tail took an elevator to the fiftieth floor. Certain he was alone, he moved down the hall and around the corner to office number 5023. He let himself in with a duplicate key having given Angel the original. After Stephen locked the door behind him, Angel turned on a desk lamp. Laid out on the couch was everything they'd need to transform Stephen Thatcher into the Moon Man.

"I wish we would have had time to test it," Angel said, fitting the battery pack to Stephen's back, under his cape.

Making sure his belt was properly adjusted, the Moon Man pressed the button on his round chrome pushed buckle.

"Testing. Testing," the Moon Man said.

A squeal like a strangled cat ripped through the small room. Angel lifted the Moon Man's cape and adjusted the volume on the battery pack.

"Testing. Testing," the Moon Man tried again.

The voice emanating from the miniature speaker sounded as if it had been strained through a robot filter, alien and emotionless.

"Okay, let's try distance," the Moon Man suggested.

Angel again lifted the cape and slid a level from zero to a ten marker.

"Test-ing-ing," the Moon Man said.

The sound of his mechanical voice seemed to float and hover a few yards from the Moon Man as he were standing near the couch instead of by the desk across the room.

"Let's…increase…the-the….distance-ance." the Moon Man's voice echoed in the room.

Angel adjusted the distance level on the battery pack and dialed back the echo.

"Testing, Testing," the Moon Man tried one more time.

The robot voice was clear and strong and had the presence of having originated thirty feet from the speaker.

"Works great," Angel said. "You ready?"

The Moon Man gave Angel the thumbs up. Angel opened the door and put a hand on his friend's shoulder.

"If you need me, Boss, press the alarm button."

Again, the Moon Man gave him the thumbs up and headed toward the elevator. Angel watched him turn the corner and said a silent prayer for his friend.

The elevator ride to the seventieth floor seemed to take forever. The Moon Man disabled the overhead elevator light so when the car arrived, the doors would open onto a dark interior. The elevator eased up and shuddered into position. The doors opened slowly with a buffered exhale. Even with the heightened vision of the helmet, the Moon Man had a difficult time discerning shapes in the deep shadows of the hedge walled platform. He moved silently to his right, as per the plan he and Angel and devised. There was the sound of footsteps nearby. They sounded as if they were coming from behind him and to his left, but it was impossible to be sure given what the helmet did to sound and direction. He paused. Listened. Silence. He located the first canister and armed it. He was moving to the next one when he heard the sound of a muffled scream. He turned to see the Faceless Man, the eyes of hell blazing in undulating shadows.

"Please, don't move," the Faceless Man commanded.

Standing behind him was one of his goons. He had one monster hand clamped over Sue's mouth, the other held her shoulder in his vice-like grip. Her eyes were wide with fear and panic. Steve had rarely seen her afraid. He'd never seen her as frightened as she was now.

The Moon Man stood hands by his sides. The Faceless Man took a step forward. The Moon Man turned suddenly, his cape flaring in a wide black arc as he disappeared into the shadows.

"Stop him!" the Faceless Man yelled.

The second giant stepped out from behind an elephant topiary and went in pursuit. He was too big and clumsy to weave in and out of the twisting paths and took several wrongs turns which gave the Moon Man enough time to arm canisters two and three.

"Over here, you big lug," the Moon Man taunted.

The voice relocation device sent the Moon Man's voice behind the goon who turned and swung his massive fist, breaking the head off of a shrub sculpted giraffe.

The Moon Man moved around behind the goon, "Why don't you pick on someone your own size, you big ape."

The goon spun around once, twice and then back. He grunted something that in tone sounded like a curse but was unintelligible. The Moon Man dashed to the far corner of the garden, armed the fourth canister and eased to the opening in the hedge that provided the panoramic view of the city below. He saw the giant coming through the sway of the hedge row. When he burst into the open, he seemed confused. It took him several seconds before he saw the Moon Man standing calmly near the entrance of another hedge maze.

"Lovely night, isn't it?" the Moon Man said.

His voice seemed to come from behind the goon, who spun at its sound. Not seeing the source, he spun back to face the Moon Man. Again, the Moon Man taunted the big lug with a chuckle that sounded as if it came from just above the giant's head. As soon as he looked up, the Moon Man disappeared into the shadows of the maze. The goon caught sight of the Moon Man's cape as it disappeared behind a shrub and ran after him.

With the Moon Man's heightened vision he saw the fish pond loom into view. Running, he stepped onto a retaining rock and launched himself to a small cement maintenance step in the center of the pond. He jumped from one step to another until he bounded to the edge of the pond wall. If he'd been wearing Stephen Thatcher's shoes, he would be waist deep in water after the first leap. But with the Moon Man's specially designed gripping soles, he was as sure-footed as a Sherpa. He turned to see the giant burst through the hedge. The Moon Man waved to the big lug which made him growl like a wild animal. The goon leaned forward, dug in his heels and took off running at full speed. The goon saw the pond a second too late. The toe of his shoe clipped the pond wall. For a second it looked like he was moving in slow motion. His arms waved in panic driven windmills, as he fell; face down into the midnight dark water.

The Moon Man waited for him to get up. There was a burst of bubbles that turned the surface of the water around the goon's head into a froth of roiling foam. The goon twitched. His legs stiffened. And he did not move again.

"Please! No! Please!"

The Moon Man had to suppress the urge to go running to the sound of Sue's stricken pleas. Stop, he told himself. Concentrate. He orientated himself to the sound of the waterfall. It was physically to his left but the splashing sounded as if it were coming from in front of him.

"No! Please!"

Sue's cries sounded as if they were coming from his right, slightly behind him. He looked up into the star-filled sky, asked for God's help, and went off ahead and slightly to the right. The Faceless Man was standing in a small clearing surrounded by blooming jasmine. The remaining goon had Sue by the shoulders, holding her several feet off the ground. He swayed her back and forth as if she were a damp dish rag. Even in the dark, the Moon Man could see the twisted delight on the monster's face.

"So good of you to join us once more," the Faceless Man said.

"Have him put her down," the Moon Man said.

His voice sounded as if here coming from a short distance behind them and both the goon and the Faceless Man looked around in dismay. It took a long moment for the Faceless Man to arrive at a conclusion. The goon was clearly unsettled and kept looking over his shoulder expecting a second Moon Man to appear.

"Very clever," the Faceless Man said. "Very clever indeed."

"Thank you, Anton. Coming from you, that's a great compliment."

At the sound of his own name, the Faceless Man's eye flared in sparks of rage.

"Mist compression with pulse sensor-driven luminescent pigment," the Moon Man said. "The condensation drip on your shoes that night at the Ballroom gave it away. That, and the small pressure tank strapped to your back under your cape. Ingenious."

"Knowing who I am won't save you or your lady friend, Moon Man. After tonight, this city will be mine."

The Faceless Man nodded to the giant who lowered Sue to the ground but did not release her.

"Remove your weapon and place it on the ground and then step forward," the Faceless man instructed. "Any heroics and my friend will toss Miss McEwen off the roof. There won't be much of her to recognize when she explodes from the impact. Trust me, I've seen what happens. If you cooperate, my friend will do you the kindness of snapping her neck. She'll never feel a thing."

The Moon Man removed the gun from its holster, tossed it to the ground and took a step forward.

"How did you know?" the Faceless Man asked.

"Your uncle. The cashier's cheques, the receipt for the specially made gloves with the articulated little finger. Your uncle is in a bad way, Anton. He needs your help."

"And he'll get it. He'll spend the rest of his days living like a king. Now step forward and remove your helmet. You know who I am. Its only fair I know who you are."

The Moon Man took a step forward raising his arms to the lock collar of the helmet.

"Dad!" Sue screamed.

The crack of gun fire split the night sky as a bullet ricocheted off the Moon Man's helmet. The lieutenant bolted from the elevator door toward the Moon Man. His second shot clipped the Moon Man's shoulder, twisting him to the side.

"Dad! No!"

Gil McEwen saw his daughter struggling in the grip of the giant. He stopped in his tracks trying to make sense of what was before his eyes. The Moon Man and the Faceless Man working together?

Sue bent forward as much as she was able and put all her strength into a backward kick, sending her heel hard into the goon's groin. He laughed.

"If you take another step," the Faceless Man said, "I'll have him break her in two."

McEwen froze.

The Moon Man eased his hand to his belt buckle, found the detonation button and pressed it. Four small pops sounded in sequence. Almost immediately, a thick fog rolled along the ground, through brushes, around flower pots, seeping through and around everything in its path. McEwen was the first to feel its effects. He staggered trying to keep his balance. Down to one knee…then both knees. Now, on his hands and knees trying not to breath, but breathing deeply and rapidly despite himself; collapsing to the gravel pathway.

The giant blinked as if it would clear the encroaching unconsciousness. He rolled his head and bellowed like a wounded animal. He picked up Sue and began to sway drunkenly, breaking through the hedge, knocking over planters and topiary. Sue screamed as they headed to the ledge.

The Moon Man turned. The bullet from the Faceless Man's .45 caught him just above his hip bone and spun him to the ground. The Moon Man rolled toward the downed lieutenant. He grabbed the gun from McEwen's hand, turned on his back and fired. The Faceless Man dodged to his right. The bullet creased his back, tearing a hole in his compression tank. When he turned back to face the Moon Man, the red eyes of hell were gone. The undulating void of a shadow that concealed his face was gone. In their place was a savaged, twisted knot of scarred flesh. His one eye, lidless and terrible, stared at the Moon Man with all-consuming hatred.

Another terrifying scream made them both look in its direction.

"Sue! Sue!" the Moon Man yelled in desperation.

There was the sound of concrete smashing apart. The wrench of twisting metal. The howl of a wild animal and the heavy thud of a massive beast exploding onto the pavement seven hundred feet below.

Anton turned at the horrific sound. When he spun to face the Moon Man, he glared at him with murderous rage. He took several steps toward the Moon Man, aiming the barrel of the gun at the Moon Man's chest. He fired four shots with each advancing step. The Moon Man convulsed as the bullets tore into his shirt front, sending rendered bits of fabric into the cool night air.

Aton stood over the Moon Man, a haggard gnarl of a smile spread across his misshapen mouth.

"This city belongs to me, Moon Man, whoever you are."

As Anton leaned over to remove the Moon Man's helmet, Stephen raised the gun, pressed it under Anton's chin and emptied the clip. Bits of his skull and brains landed in the fish pond and were eagerly consumed.

The Moon Man found Sue unconscious in a bed of petunias. A four-foot section of retaining wall had been broken through. Among the rubble was a small, wide brimmed hat.

The Moon Man carried Sue to the elevator. The pain in his side from the gun shot and the impact of the bullets fired against his bullet proof vest at such a close range made him light headed. The elevator doors opened on the fiftieth floor. There was Angel, jabbing his finger at the UP button. When he saw Stephen and Sue, he burst into tears of joy. He helped them out of the elevator, eased Sue to the floor and helped the Moon Man out of his helmet. The rush of cool fresh air against Stephen's face revived him a little.

"You had me worried," Angel said.

"I had *me* worried," Stephen smiled. "Let's get out of here before Gil comes looking for us."

"The lieutenant?"

"Long story, my friend," Stephen said. "One hell of a long strange story."

"So let me get this straight," Angel said.

Sue, Stephen and Angel were sitting on the balcony of Stephen's house. Birds were singing in the trees. A light breeze brought in the scent of freshly mown hay from the fields that surrounded Stephens property. They were on their second pot of coffee. A nearly empty bag of fresh pastries lay at the center of the table. Blackie, a wild crow that had acquired a fondness for baked goods, enjoyed stealing bits of crumbs as he hopped from plate to plate.

"This Anton Corbin guy invents the Faceless Man and commits those robberies to take care of his ailing uncle?"

"Well, yes," Stephen said, "But there's much more to it."

"I'd say to him," Angel said, "hey buddy, get a job. I supported my family working as a bouncer before I got into the ring,"

"You know about the Corbin murder case?" Stephen asked.

"Who doesn't?" Sue replied.

"Jasper Corbin was arrested for the double homicide," Stephen continued. "His brother, William, was convicted. Somehow, Jasper's nephew, Anton, knew the truth about what his father had done. He made the mistake of telling his father he wanted to go to the police with what he knew. That's when William set his own son on fire."

"Oh my God," Sue was horrified.

"So, he wasn't whisked off to Argentina because he was linked to a drowning?" Angel conjectured. "He was taken there to save the boy from his father?"

"The world's leading specialist in burn reconstructive surgery lives in Buenos Aries," Stephen added.

"He looked like that after the surgery?" Sue was trying to imagine the horror of it.

"After dozens of them," Stephen explained. "Anton's father was a viscious, sadistic man. Whatever mental breakdown turned Anton to a life of crime was due to the way he was abused by his own dad."

"Terrible," Sue added. "Just terrible."

"One good thing has come out of all this," Stephen said.

"Yeah?" Angel cocked an eyebrow.

"Lieutenant Gilbert McEwen is a hero and he's had to admit that he was wrong about the Charity Ball and Museum robberies. The Moon Man wasn't responsible."

"McEwen a hero?" Angel sneered derisively. "The only reason that lunatic isn't running the city is because of the Moon Man. All the lieutenant did was show up and pass out."

"You know that. Sue knows that. And I know that."

"But daddy thinks he saved the day." Sue had a pretty smile on her face. "But that's daddy, isn't it?"

Sue and Stephen looked at each other for a long moment.

"And something else good came out of it too," she said beaming. She lifted her left hand and turned it toward Angel. An engagement ring with a diamond so big and bright, Blackie the crow, titled his head, considering his options.

"Congratulations, you guys!" Angel said, raising his coffee cup for a toast.

They clinked cups.

"Ah, just think," Angel said. "Soon there'll be the patter of little Moon Man feet."

Sue crunched up her napkin and threw it at him.

THE END

WRITING THE MOON MAN

I wanted to open with a scene that would put all but one of the major characters together in the same place, witness the same event and then watch them react, in character, throughout the story. I had a vague idea of what the villain was going to be with the first draft. Who he was, was revealed to me, and in turn the reader, near the end of the story with a casually spoken line by Detective Stephen Thatcher after reading the note from Arthur Stanslensy, the glove maker.

"Missing little finger," Stephen said absently.

I won't have been the first writer to credit his characters for shaping the storyline. They reveal themselves to you, and as they do, the story unfolds. I liked the visual of the Faceless Man and his two giant goons. Without them, he's just another guy in a goofy looking costume. He hasn't any powers. There's nothing dangerous or intimidating about him. But with them, he has power. And he uses that power for evil. It wasn't until he and Stephen are face to faceless that I had to deal with the physicality of how the Faceless Man created the effect of being faceless. When Stephen looked down and saw the drop of condensation on the Faceless Man's shoe, I had my answer, and the method of his unmasking.

Right from the beginning we know who Sue is. She's hard working, selfless, considerate and the dame has Moxie. She demurs at Stephen's praise of her putting the gala together and steps up in Sister Mary Catherine's defense as the nun is confronted by the Faceless Man. Throughout the story she's brave and caring. Even on the observation platform, being held by one of the goons, she shows what she's made of with a kick to the big lug's family jewels. Its only when things begin to look hopeless, does she give into fear.

I thought it was important to make a clear difference between Stephen and the Moon Man. We know they're the same man, but when Stephen is the Moon Man, not only does he wear the hero's armor but his perceptions and reactions are changed because of it.

I usually write in the morning. There's noting like sitting in the easy chair, fueled by several cups of good coffee and then see where the story takes me. I have a habit of presenting myself with problems and then letting possible solutions bounce around during the day, creep around in my sleep and see if—come morning—I've got them solved. What, physically, would it be like to wear the Argus glass helmet was one of those problems. There would have to be some advantages to wearing the helmet aside from concealing his identify. So, I gave him heightened vision and a sensitivity to sound. But, the downside would have to be the misdirection of sound. And at the most critical time, he's forced to deal with it.

I hadn't had the chance to read a Moon Man story before writing my own so not sure how other writers dealt with Lieutenant McEwen. To me, and to Angel, he's kind of a puffed up pain in the butt. That he's obsessed with the Moon Man can only make him less effective as a policeman. In the last scene, both Stephen and Sue acknowledge her father's character flaw while it continues to rankle Angel.

Writing *The Moon Man and the Faceless Terror* presented some interesting challenges. I liked the way it turned out. I hope you do as well.

TIM BRUCKNER - I suppose I'm best known as a sculptor. Over the past forty-five years I've produced hundreds of action figures and collectible statues for companies like DC Direct (now DC Entertainment), Side Show, Gentle Giant, Dark Horse and many more. Early in my career I created art for several album covers. Most notably the art for Ringo Starr's *Ringo* cover. Around that same time I worked as an illustrator and designer. In my late twenties I wrote, performed and produced three children's albums for Casablanca Records. Sandwiched in there were a couple of special effects projects, sculpting and art directing work on the alligator suit for the movie *Alligator*. These days I've semi-retired from commercial work, exploring my own creative projects and writing. I've been writing short stories since I was a kid. A couple of years ago I co-wrote *Pop Sculpture: how to create action figures and collectible statues*, published by Watson-Guptill. Last year I published my first book of fiction, *Sensible Redhorn*, a collection of four pulp driven stories centered around a hardnosed crime reporter. Most recently, I've had the great fortune of being able to work with Ron Fortier and Airship 27. Hold onto your seats, it's going to be a pulpy ride! Visit my site at www.timbruckner.com and visit me at Facebook for the latest news.

INVASION : GREAT CITY

By Terry Alexander

"**I** hate special assignments." Lieutenant Gil McEwen sipped the lukewarm coffee. His face wrinkled in disgust. "This stuff is awful." He shook his head and poured the tepid liquid into the gutter.

"Why did we get selected to babysit this bunch?" Detective-Sergeant Stephen Thatcher shifted from one foot to the other, watching a line of workers streaming inside the Great City Friendship Hall. "I don't understand why the Mayor allowed the Bund to have a convention here. Once these guys get a foothold in a city they're as hard to shake as a bad cold."

"Great City needs the income. The Chief has the whole department stretched thin. Everyone is pulling special duty because of this rally." Gil patted his pocket searching for a cigarette. "Haven't smoked in years, and I still get the urge to light up."

"Dad's not happy with the Mayor's decision. The rally will bring a lot of money in, and Great City can use the dough. But I don't understand how Fritz Kuhn and the American Nazi Party can support Hitler after he signed a non-aggression pact with Russian. The Bund is strictly non-communist."

"Will you look at that?" Gil shook his head. "A painting of George Washington and Adolf side by side, talk about strange bedfellows."

"They have a painting of him and Hitler at every rally. They're desperate to make a connection with the first President." Stephen shrugged. "They sure hired a lot of workmen for this rally."

"They're expecting ten thousand people here over the weekend." Gil shook his head. "Every city that's hosted one of these rallies has had problems with this bunch. Trouble follows them where ever they go."

"With the situation in Europe, this will likely be the final one. Hitler may have been voted Time Magazine's Man of the Year in 38, but after the invasion of Poland, people are beginning to see through his lies."

"We'll be in a shooting war with the krauts before you know it." Gil grabbed Stephen's sleeve. "My God, look at that." His eyes bulged in excitement. "That's one of the new Pontiac Silver Streamliners. That is a beautiful car, has the new straight eight under the hood."

Stephen smiled. "Gil you know a lot about that model. Why don't you buy one?"

"On my salary," he grunted. "Are you kidding?"

"Hey, they have a chauffeur and everything." Stephen frowned. "That's odd, a driver for a Pontiac."

"That's Fritz Kuhn, the man who's throwing this shindig. His followers call him the American Fuhrer. The dame has some nice gams. Wish I could see her face." Gil turned to the younger officer. "Remember, be polite."

Stephen stared at the well-dressed man and the veiled mystery woman. She waited at the curb and took Kuhn's arm and allowed him to lead her up the concrete steps toward the huge oak doors of the Friendship Hall.

"Mister Kuhn." Gil nodded. "Miss, pleasure to see you both. Everything seems to be moving right on schedule."

"Thank you, Lieutenant." Kuhn shook Gil's hand. "Allow me to introduce Miss Monique Carmon. She arrived this morning from Germany to lend her support."

"My Pleasure." Gil bowed slightly. "This is Detective-Sergeant Stephen Thatcher."

A gust of wind caught the edge of her white veil and sent it fluttering above her chin, giving Stephen a glimpse at her smooth flawless skin. "I am honored to meet you both." She turned to her companion. "Fritz, will this building be large enough to meet our needs?" she asked.

"I believe it will do nicely." Kuhn smiled. "Come inside, let me show you around." He turned to the officers. "I have some workmen coming from Chicago. I have plans for a custom made podium. Please direct them inside." His arm interlocked with the veiled woman. Her shapely hips swished from side to side, as the pair disappeared inside.

"Can't stand that guy," Stephen whispered. "But, the woman seems familiar."

"How could you tell anything about her, with that veil?" Gil frowned.

Stephen snapped his finger. "The Bly case in Detroit, didn't it mention something about a woman wearing a veil?"

"Don't start jumping to conclusions." Gil glanced from the driver, beside the Pontiac, and the entrance to the Friendship Hall. His eyes twinkled with excitement. "I'm going inside for a few minutes. Talk to the chauffeur and see if he knows anything."

Stephen nodded. He jammed his hands in his pockets and walked slowly down the stairs. "How are you doing?" He glanced at the head of the stairs, the lieutenant nodded slightly and turned toward the door. "Do you have to stand at attention until Kuhn returns?"

The driver's eyes shifted to the detective and back to the stairs. "I can't speak to anyone when I'm on duty, one of Mr. Kuhn's rules." He spoke with a mid-western accent.

"You must have had a busy day. Did you meet Miss Carmon at the dock?"

The nervous driver licked his lips. "What are you talking about? We picked her up at the train station bout an hour ago. Go away, will yah? If the boss sees me talking to anyone, he'll fire me for sure."

"Sorry, Mac, don't want to spoil a good thing." Stephen touched his index finger to his brow and ambled down the sidewalk. A fiery red *Ford* convertible pulled to a stop beside the curb. "What are you up to, good looking?" Sue McEwen opened the door and ran to Stephen's arms, her mass of curls a shade darker than the convertible.

"What are you doing here?" Stephen squeezed her tightly and planted a discreet kiss on her lips.

"I wanted to see you for a few moments," she whispered. "Get your mind off this depressing assignment. I can't understand how anyone in America can willingly follow that madman. Don't they read the papers; don't they know about the forced labor camps and the experiments he's conducting on people?"

"Sue, those are rumors, none of it's been proven." Stephen grabbed her hand walking toward the stairs. "Your dad's inside. He wanted a word with Mr. Kuhn."

"Kuhn's a louse and a muckraker." Her gaze centered on the driver standing by the streamliner satisfied he was out of ear shot. She leaned in close to Stephen's ear. "I saw Angel earlier. He's tailing a couple of workmen."

"Any idea if he found anything?"

She smiled and shook her head. To a casual passer-by viewing their conversation, they appeared to be two young lovers whispering sweet promises of affection to one another. In fact, they shared a secret, one that if known would condemn Stephen to life behind prison walls.

"Sue, you shouldn't come here and distract your fiancé when he's working." The stern voice of Gil McEwen sounded from the stairs. "You two were so absorbed in your conversation I could have walked right past you with a Tommy gun, and you wouldn't have noticed."

"I'm meeting Angel tonight after my shift's over," Stephen nodded.

Sue broke away from his embrace and ran to her father. "Dad," she threw her arms around his neck. "I got lonely, and decided to check on my two favorite guys. Don't be cross with me."

"I can't stay mad at you." His dour face broke into a smile. "But I don't want you hanging out down here. I don't trust these Nazis."

Her lips stretched into a pout. "Well, I know when I'm not wanted." She said in a pseudo-hurt voice.

"Don't try that puppy dog look with me young lady. You're not a little girl anymore." Gil glanced at the driver, standing ramrod stiff by the Pontiac. "These guys are dangerous. I just don't want you to be in harm's way."

"Your dad's right, Sue." Stephen pulled his fiancé to his side. "You really shouldn't put yourself in danger." He squeezed her hand.

"At least the Moon Man has been quiet for a few days." Gil nodded. "I'd hate to be dealing with that crook and watching the bund at the same time."

"Thank goodness." Sue snuggled Stephen's side. "Walk me back to my car, Handsome. Drop by the house when you get off."

"Afraid that's out of the question." Gil waved goodbye to his daughter. "We won't get relieved until midnight."

Ned 'Angel' Dargan crouched in the shadows of the abandoned Monarch warehouse. The derelict structure was one of many scattered throughout the city used by the Moon Man in his fight against crime. A loud board screeched on the rickety staircase. Angel held his breath, waiting for the second signal. Five seconds later the screech sounded again. The ex-boxer picked up a small hammer and whacked the water-pipes behind him. A metallic sound rang throughout the warehouse.

A dark suited man, wearing a black cloak walked into the room. A shaft of moonlight passed through the broken window and reflected off the globe of Argus glass that completely covered his face.

"Any news, Angel?" The bowl distorted his voice.

"I watched those guys all day like you said. They walked around like they were tourists instead of workmen." Angel scratched his crooked nose that was broken years ago in the ring. A drunken doctor set it improperly, leaving it permanently bent with an odd lump on the bridge.

"Did they pay attention to any specific area?"

"The Rosenfeld Market. They walked around that place for nearly an hour. They were interested in the back door deliveries," Angel mumbled. "I don't like these guys boss. They make my skin crawl, and I've spent time in some real hellholes."

"I'll drive by the market tonight and see if anyone's sniffing around." The bizarrely dressed man pulled a wad of greenbacks from his coat. "This is five hundred. Deliver it to Mrs. Jameson on Fourth and DuPont. Her mother recently died, and she needs to pay for a funeral and two months of past due rent."

"I gotcha, Boss." Angel stuffed the money in his threadbare jacket.

"Be at the worksite at five in the morning. Avoid the police but keep your eyes on those two workmen, if they leave, follow them and report back here tomorrow night."

"I can do that," Dargan nodded.

"Angel, have your contacts mentioned a veiled woman coming to Great City?"

The haggard face settled into a frown. "No, but I'll keep my ears open."

"Keep fifty dollars for yourself. Pay your rent and buy some food." The glass shifted forward slightly. "You're looking a little thin."

"Thanks." Angel climbed wearily to his feet. "I'll see you here tomorrow."

"Tomorrow." The masked man disappeared into the shadows.

Angel Dargan waited for ten minutes, giving his boss and benefactor ample time to leave the building before he moved. He slowly walked the back stairs leading to the secret entrance. He had a lot to do before morning.

Angel stifled a yawn, he leaned against the alley wall of Durants Clothiers across the street from the Great City Friendship Hall. Several workmen gathered on the ornate stone stairs, although he couldn't hear their words, from their wild gestures it was a heated discussion.

Five minutes later a blue *Ford* sedan stopped near the sidewalk. He recognized the two detectives that climbed from the vehicle. "More cops," he mumbled.

The workmen waited, while the construction supervisor unlocked the Friendship Hall. Two workmen stopped at the entrance, Angel watched as one patted his pockets as if he were looking for a missing item. Their supervisor appeared at the door. A mumble of voices came to his ears. Seconds later the pair turned and bolted down the steps.

"Where are you boys going?" Angel jammed his hands in his ragged jacket and moved from his place of concealment following the pair at a safe distance. Traffic was light, only an occasional passer-by moved about at this early hour.

The pair turned at the corner, walked half a block and crossed the street. Angel kept walking, giving the two men ample time to get well ahead. They paused at a bakery, noses tipped in the air as the scent of fresh baked bread drifted on the breeze.

Damn it, they're suspicious. Despite the cool early morning air, a sweaty film covered Angel's forehead. He passed the bread store on the opposite side of the street and turned at the next corner. He pressed his back against the brick front of Osmond's Jewelry and waited.

Come on, Fellas, don't keep me waiting. He licked his lips nervously. After fifteen minutes the men continued their journey. They paused at the corner, crossed the street and kept walking. *I don't like this. Something's not right.* He waited patiently, his right foot propped on the wall. When the men neared the next corner Angel pushed himself away from the outer wall. His brisk pace ate up the distance. He crossed the street at the next corner, hoping to get a glimpse of the men ahead.

Blast it, where did they go? He broke into a trot, his worn shoes slapping the sidewalk. *They can't be too far ahead.* Large paw like hands fastened on his collar as he darted past a dark alley mouth.

"What are you doing, you little snoop?" A nasally voice sounded in his ear a moment before stars filled his eyes.

Angel slouched forward, moving his head with the impact to lessen the power of the strike. A hard right landed in his gut. Listening to the footfalls, Angel lashed out with a tremendous uppercut. It smacked the lead attacker square on the jaw and sent the man reeling.

"You're a scrapper." A nasally tone came from his left. "I like a good brawl." A rock-hard fist slammed Angel's ear. His jaw popped from the impact.

Angel stumbled. He put all his effort in a wild looping left, the blow struck a muscular forearm. *This guy is good. He's been around the ring.*

"That is enough." The cold kiss of a gun barrel settled in the short hair behind his ear. "Put this cretin in the car," a female voice carried through the warehouse.

"At once," a shaky voice answered.

A hard fist landed in the pit of his stomach, the air burst from Angel's lungs. Slumping to his knees, his vision cleared as his unseen assailants forced him to the ground. His hands were yanked behind his back; a tall blonde man removed the shoestring from his worn left shoe and bound his thumbs together. "I hope I get to meet up with you again, Tough Guy," the nasally voice whispered in his ear. "I'd like to have a crack at you one on one."

"I'll try to arrange that." A line of blood drained from Angel's lip. His eyes fastened on the man's scarred mug. "Slingshot McGuire," he mumbled. "Thought I recognized the voice."

"In the car now," the woman ordered.

"Yeah, Boss."

Rough hands shoved him toward the rear door, giving Angel his first glimpse of the Veiled Lady. "You have wasted enough time here. Go to the market, I want exact times on their deliveries. I'll deal with this miscreant."

Market, they're going back to Rosenfeld's. Angel focused on the small caliber pistol leveled at his middle. "Don't lose my shoe, it's the only pair I have." He slowly climbed into the back seat of the dark sedan.

"That's the least of your worries." The shapely woman nudged him with the pistol and climbed in the back seat. "I need a special place for this one," she said to the driver. "Take us to a quiet location by the riverfront. I don't want anyone to hear his screams."

"J. Edgar ain't happy about this latest Bund rally." Paulie 'the Bear' Grogan paced back and forth in front of Blake Manner's sofa. "Great City is a tinder box, and the American Nazis may be the match that'll burn the place to the ground."

"I can't travel across the country." Blake shook his head. "My editor's not gonna go for that, the Daily Sun has a limited budget."

"Your supervisor has capable men assigned to the east coast." Amazona curled her shapely legs on the cushions. "Why doesn't he just send a team of agents to deal with the Bund?"

"With the tension in Europe and the prospect of foreign spies prowling the states, Mr. Hoover doesn't want to pull any agents from the field." Paulie ran his stubby fingers through his hair. "He sent me here to ask for your help, Great City has unique problems. Hoods behind every corner and they have this nut running around with a fish bowl on his head."

A frown creased Amazona's comely features. "That sounds like a very uncomfortable choice in garments."

"I've heard about that guy. Calls himself the Moon Man." Blake rose from the couch shaking his head. "I'd like to help, and I'd love to get the story, but my editor is a real skinflint and he won't foot the bill for this."

"We need you and Amazona on this." Paulie scraped his beefy jowls. "She may be the only one with the raw power to handle this assignment."

The dark haired beauty jumped to her feet, intertwining her arm with Manners. "I won't go without Blake." She nodded. "You can tell Mr. Hoover that."

"Talk to your boss," Paulie mumbled. "Plant the seed; I'll see what I can do on my end to pull this thing together." He jammed his hat atop his head, and left, slamming the door in his wake.

"Are you going to speak with Mister Chambers?" Amazona asked.

"First thing in the morning." Blake smiled. "But I promised you a night of dancing and romance."

"Give me fifteen minutes." She grabbed her shoes and ran to the bedroom. "I've got the perfect dress."

Where is Angel? Stephen Thatcher stared down the sidewalk. The two workmen who left earlier that morning returned at noon. But the former pugilist never reappeared at his post across the street. A nervous flame burned in his stomach. He knew Angel would never ignore his instructions.

Something's happened. Those two must have seen him and realized he was tailing them. Stephen licked his lips. He gritted his teeth in frustration, he had to do something. Steve glanced at his pocket watch, six hours until the meeting with Angel. While Lieutenant McEwen didn't approve of their current assignment, he took his responsibilities seriously and wouldn't allow him to leave without a good reason.

Stephen pulled a toothpick from his pocket and jammed it in his mouth. He checked his pocket watch for the tenth time. It was nearly two-thirty. *Where are you, Angel?*

"Why were you following my men?" The Veiled Lady stood before him, his eyes fastened on the split in her dress that ran to her thigh, displaying a pair of shapely legs.

"You've got a great voice, toots, real sexy." Angel nodded. "I didn't notice earlier because my vision was blurry, but you have a fine set of gams. Cut me loose and we can go dancing tonight." He struggled against his bonds. The mysterious woman had replaced the shoestring around his thumbs with strands of tough rope. He strained against his bonds, chaffing his wrists.

"Idiot." She slapped him hard across the face. "Tell me why you were following my men?"

Angel spit blood at her feet. "You hit harder than Slingshot, that's for sure." He smiled showing scarlet teeth. "Actually, I wuz planning on rolling those two. They got a job so they had to have a little folding money on them."

A stifled laugh came from behind the veil. "Don't take me for a fool. Are you working for the police?"

"Lady, you're nuts. I don't trust the peelers, as far as I could throw one of the bums." He stared at the white veil hanging beneath the ornate pink hat. "I'm giving you the straight dope here, I wuz gonna pick up a few bucks from your boys, my rent is due tomorrow and I don't have two nickels to rub together."

She turned to her driver. "Kill him, make it quick. I'll be in the car."

The burly man pulled a pistol from his waistband. "My pleasure." His face split into a gap toothed grin.

"Whoa, hold the phone there sweetheart." The rushed words ran together. "We need to talk this over."

"There is nothing to discuss." She turned to her driver. "Don't keep me waiting long." The veiled Lady passed through the door. A brilliant shaft of sunlight flashed in the driver's eyes, blinding him for a moment.

Angel jumped to his feet. He raced through the cluttered warehouse in a lopsided gait. *Wish I had both shoes. If that punk back there doesn't kill me, I'll step on a rusty nail and get tetanus.*

A bullet buzzed past his ear, lifting his hair. *Damn, that was close.* Angel circled a pile of discarded lumber, seeking to find safety. *Where are we?*

He strained against the ropes binding his wrists, gaining a little slack. Angel saw a shaft of daylight streaming through a partially covered window on the second floor. A dust covered, rickety staircase came into view. He raced toward the wooden structure, desperate to make it upstairs before the gunman caught up with him. A second bullet splattered a stack of lumber to his left. Sharp splinters ripped through his thin shirt and peppered his flesh.

He's gonna get lucky in a second, I've got to find a way out of here. He bounded up the steps three at a time, his foot slipped on the second floor landing. For a moment he balanced precariously on the edge.

A burning pain erupted in Angel's right thigh. He fell to his knees; a warm liquid trickled down his leg. Angel glanced down the staircase, the shooter stood at the bottom lining up the kill shot. He rolled across the floor, as the bullet pinged over his head.

Angel struggled to his feet. He gained some additional slack in the rope. He tried to run but settled on a step-hop gait. *Where's that damned window?* A shaft of light appeared on the floor before him. Forcing himself forward, he kicked at the covered panes. The glass shattered under his remaining shoe.

A sizable retaining pond, full of green stagnant water lay fifteen feet from the warehouse. He glanced at the driver slowly coming up the stairs, his mouth curled in an evil smirk.

"I'm gonna enjoy this." The driver cocked the hammer.

Angel backed to the edge of the catwalk and ran forward. Flaming tendrils of pain shot through his leg. He placed all his weight on his good leg and pushed off from the window ledge. *Hope that pool's deep enough to hide me. What if they threw scrap in there?* A vision of himself impaled on a length of rusty pipe filled his mind as he curled into a ball and enter the pool with a tremendous splash.

Where is he? The Moon Man tugged the pocket watch free. He moved to a sliver of moonlight and glared at the unmoving hands. It was a quarter till four. *If they've hurt Angel, I'll hunt them all down and make them pay.*

The screech of wood on the staircase interrupted his vow of vengeance. The Moon Man counted the seconds, waiting for the prearranged signal. At the appropriate time, the high pitched squeal sounded again.

Lifting the hammer he banged on the pipes. *That has to be Angel.* Fighting back the instinct to check on his friend, the Moon Man waited in the darkness. He drew his .45 and cocked the hammer as the bizarre step drag sound grew louder.

The door opened with a squeal of rusty hinges. Angel stood framed in the doorway, soaking wet, blood oozing from his injuries. "They took me down by the docks, the old Wilson Processing Plant. Tried their best to kill me, but I managed to get away." He fell to his knees. His shoulders quivered with every rasping breath. "They're gonna hit the Rosenfeld Market when the old man is getting his morning deliveries." He collapsed on his face.

"Angel." The Moon Man covered the distance in three steps. Moonlight glinted from the Argus globe atop his head. He rolled Angel to his back and cradled his head in his lap. "Who did this?"

"You wuz right about the veiled dame. She's in charge of those two workmen. They pinched me, she ordered her driver to kill me, and he surely did try. I managed to jump into the retaining pond behind the building. My lungs wuz nearly busting before he stopped shooting into the water." Angel sucked a deep breath into his lungs. "Get to the market. You've got to save Rosenfeld."

"What about you? You need medical attention."

"Don't worry about me boss, but if you run into a big guy that talks through his nose, blast him." Angel sagged like dead weight in his arms.

The Moon Man gently lowered Angel's head to the trash covered floor. Gloved hands pulled the pocket watch from his jacket. Rosenfeld met his deliveries at five in the morning, giving him just over an hour to get there and stop the Veiled Lady's plan.

He raced down the stairs, pausing at the side entrance to the old warehouse to ensure no one was about. Nimble fingers released the catch at the back of the elaborate mask. He removed the cloak and wrapped the globe in its folds. Stephen Thatcher hurried down the alley to his waiting roadster. Taking a moment to pack his costume in the trunk, he jumped behind the wheel. The engine started easily. He popped the clutch and peeled away.

Got to find a phone, get hold of Sue. She can sneak away and help Angel. He jammed his foot to the floor, the vehicle accelerated through a red light as he sped toward Rosenfeld's Market. Stephen spied a street light on the corner of John Dover and Pine Street, its bright illumination shining down on a glass enclosed phone booth.

Stephen stamped hard on the brake. Smoke rose from the tires, as the roadster lurched to a stop. Nervous hands fumbled with the door handle. He ran for the phone, searching his pockets for change. His fingers closed on a single dime, feeding the coin into the slot. "Operator, get me Riverside 652," he said.

"Angel, who did this?"

"One moment." The phone began to ring.

Come on, Sue. Pick up, pick up.

"Hullo," a sleepy voice answered after the eighth ring. "Who is this? What time is it anyway?"

"It's Steve." He blurted the words. "Angel's at the warehouse on Canal Street. He's in a bad way and needs help."

"What?" The tired slur disappeared from Sue's voice. "When did he get hurt?"

"This afternoon." Stephen's rapid speech slowed to a normal cadence. "Take him to a doctor or the hospital. Just get him some help."

"It'll take me a half hour to get to the warehouse." Sue answered with the same urgent tone. "I'll take care of him."

"I'll talk to you tomorrow. I'm going to the Rosenfeld Market. Something bad is going to happen, and I've got to try and stop it."

"Be careful, Darling. I love you."

"Love you too." Stephen slammed the phone into the receiver. He jumped over the passenger door and squirmed into the driver's seat. The engine roared to life and sped down the road, leaving drifting smoke in its wake.

Stephen parked the roadster two blocks away from Rosenfeld's. He pulled the watch from his coat. *Ten minutes, I've got ten minutes before the first delivery.* He inserted the key in the trunk latch and turned, pressing the silver button. *I don't like the Moon Man being out on the streets this close to dawn.*

He pulled the cloak and globe free and raced down the street, hoping he could find a nearby alley to don the trappings of his other persona. Sweat trickled down his forehead, collecting around his eyes and mouth. He spied an alley catty-corner from the market. Disappearing inside the darkness, Stephen drew the cloak across his shoulders. Taking a second to cool off from his recent excretions, he inhaled several deep breaths to reduce his body heat, lest the inside of his Argus glass mask fog over.

Satisfied, he settled the one-way dome over his head and snapped it into place. *Now I've got to work my way to the back of the store and wait.*

He drew his .45, ready to dash across the street. Before he had an opportunity to put his shaky plan into action, a large canvas-covered flatbed slowed in front of the store and turned into the delivery entrance.

The Moon Man hesitated, as the truck rounded the corner, parking at the rear of the market. *Damn, I'm not in position.* Hard soled shoes rang on the asphalt. The sound of gunshots shattered the early morning darkness.

A large man stood over the bloody body of Moe Rosenfeld, smoking gun gripped in his fist. He glared at The Moon Man as he burst into the alley. "What the hell are you doing here?" Scarred puffy lips pulled away in a snarl. The pistol moved like a living thing, centering on the Moon Man's chest.

A bullet plucked at his shoulder, boring through the cloak. The Moon Man dropped to one knee. He lined up his shot and squeezed the trigger. The burly man stumbled from the bullet's impact; a red rose blossomed on his chest. The killer drew a rattling breath and collapsed on his face.

"Damn You, Hank was a friend of mine," a nasally voice shouted from the delivery truck.

Hot lead zipped past the Argus glass mask. *That has to be Slingshot McGuire.* With calm deliberation the Moon Man sighted down the barrel. His finger tightened on the trigger. "This is for Angel," he mumbled.

An earth shaking explosion rocked the store. Debris flew into the sky and rained down on the Moon Man. A jagged length of lumber struck the glass bowl, sharp pointed nails gouged the globe, breaking a small chunk away near his right eye.

The masked man shook his head. The automatic near his fist blurred in and out of focus. Shaking hands circled the weapon, squeezing the grip. He glanced at the flaming litter scattered throughout the delivery area, hoping to find Slingshot McGuire. The hood vanished in the confusion. The Moon Man raced from the inferno

A camera flashed from the alley mouth. He caught a glimpse of a gray-haired man wearing a tee shirt and boxers with street shoes, the flash obscured his face. *Damn, hope he's not a professional. I don't want to see my picture on the afternoon edition.*

"Blake, have you seen this story from Great City." Amazona ran to the breakfast table, her open robe showing her shapely thighs. "It's a picture of the Moon Man running from a flaming grocery." She flopped into the straight-backed wooden chair, her mused dark hair cascaded around her shoulders.

Blake nodded. "I've seen it, Paulie called when the news hit the wires. Then Mr. Chambers when he received the picture. He's okayed the trip to Great City." A smile split the reporter's face. "I have to bring a bang up story back, one that'll go nation-wide."

She returned his smile. "When do we leave?"

"As soon as you pack." Blake sipped at his coffee and popped a piece of toast in his mouth. "He nearly choked on his words, but Chambers promised me two seats on a *Boeing 247,* leaving for *New York* at noon. We'll take the train to Great City. If I've figured it right, we should arrive about midnight."

Amazona's brown eyes sparkled. "This is wonderful news. Have you told Paulie?"

"Going to call him now. We'll need his connections to deal with the police."

Amazona jumped from the table. She circled to Blake and planted a long passionate kiss on his lips. "I'm going to pack." She ran to the bedroom.

Stephen Thatcher and Sue McEwen waited anxiously at the Great City train depot. His father, the Chief of Police, ordered a police escort for the visiting newshound and his lady-friend, coming to Great City to report on the German American Bund and the firebombing of the Rosenfeld Market.

He glanced at the bright light of the approaching locomotive. "Blast that photographer, now I'm babysitting reporters. I should be looking for Slingshot McGuire. He's the only lead I have in the Rosenfeld's murder."

Sue squeezed his hand lightly. "I'll help anyway I can."

Stephen nodded. "Thanks, Sue. I'll need it, with Angel out of action. Thankfully he'll recover."

She smiled. "I'm glad to hear that. I hope we like these people."

"They're taking me away from the investigation."

The air brakes hissed, steam billowed from the decelerating engine. The huffing locomotive lurched to a stop beside the platform. "Great City," a porter screamed. "Everyone off for Great City."

A man and woman stepped from the passenger car. All eyes immediately focused on the female, tall, with raven black hair and dark eyes. Her features appeared to be carved fine marble. She moved with the sensuous graceful ease of a jungle cat.

Stephen felt a vice like grip squeezing his hand. He turned to look at Sue and swallowed the hard lump in his throat. "I think that's the couple we're supposed to meet," she said.

"Yeah, you're right." They walked forward, slowly. "Are you Blake Manners and Amazona?" Stephen asked.

"That's us." Blake nodded. He offered his hand. "This is Amazona."

Blake's hard grip surprised Stephen. "I'm Stephen Thatcher and this is Sue McEwen." The pressure on his hand increased. "My fiancé." He added.

The pressure eased somewhat.

"What's your last name?" Sue glanced at the tall woman.

"My people only have one name." Amazona's eyes sparkled as she shook hands with Stephen and Sue. "I am very pleased to meet you both."

"I've got a car at the corner. The Chief made arrangements to place you at the Carlton, best hotel in town." Stephen jerked his head toward the parking lot.

"I live there, myself," Sue added quickly.

"What's your opinion of the German American Bund holding a rally in your fair city?" Blake asked.

"Darling," Amazona cooed, "don't put the detective on the spot. You can become the crusading reporter in the morning."

"Sorry, force of habit," Blake said. "You said the car was this way."

"Let me help you with the luggage," Stephen offered.

Sue reluctantly released his hand and fell into step beside Amazona, letting Stephen and Blake take the lead. "What country are you from?" she asked. "I've never heard of a country where people don't have last names."

Amazona turned and met the shorter woman's eyes. "I'm the last of my kind, my people were stranded in the arctic. Blake found his way to our settlement. I fell in love with him instantly and followed him to his sailing ship, after we freed it from the ice. We sailed back to the United States."

Sue forehead wrinkled, as she stared at the strange woman.

"The detective is your fiancé?" Amazona asked.

"Yes, we've been engaged for a year."

"Have you discussed a date?"

"Stephen wants to wait until the city is safe." Sue answered. They both agreed to place marriage on hold until Great City no longer needed the Moon Man.

"He is a very idealistic man. Will the city ever truly be safe? The entire world could go to war at any time."

"That's why he wants to wait." Sue nodded. "You're right about Steve; he is a very driven idealistic man. Here's the car."

"Climb in, ladies." Stephen slammed the trunk. "Next stop, The Hotel Carlton."

"Your people, ready to move?" The female silhouette behind the beaded curtain, struggled with the words. "We must control Great City."

"The Fuhrer and Prime Minister Tojo are very interested in this operation." Fritz Kuhn walked into the light. "If we succeed, the entire world will be under Axis control before the year is out."

The Veiled Lady glanced at the American Fuhrer, she crossed her legs, showing ample thigh. "You hired me to do a job and I'm very good at my work. If you doubt me, I'll take my people and leave this burg."

"That's not necessary." The shadowy figure stood, a small Asian woman parted the screen and walked to Kuhn's side. Her skin flawless, her dark hair tied back behind her ears. She wore a red dress with a yellow sash around her waist. "Prime Minister has agreed to your price."

"Madame Terror, nice to see you again. My men will hit the train yard tonight." The Veiled Lady's sultry voice echoed through the room. "It'll look like a massive robbery gone wrong. We'll destroy as much track and railway cars as possible. When the workmen start arriving, your men should be able to blend in. The cops will be so busy they won't notice a few extras wandering around, that'll give you time to set your plan into motion."

"Timing is everything in this operation." Kuhn took Madame Terror's hand and led her toward the door. "I've seen the papers. The police are blaming the Moon Man for Monday's explosion. We can use this to our advantage."

"His interference cost me some good men. I hope he shows up again. My men will kill him for certain." Her hot breath pushed the veil from her face, showing her lower jaw. "Just wait for the extra edition of tomorrow's paper."

Stephen Thatcher helped Blake and Amazona unload their luggage and walked them to the elevators. "I'm on duty at the Friendship Hall tomorrow. Come by and look around. You may get a comment from Fritz Kuhn."

"The American Fuhrer, yeah, a statement from him would really make my story." He leaned forward and pressed the lobby button. "I'll see you tomorrow."

"Hold the elevator for a moment," Sue said. "I want to walk Stephen to the door." She grabbed his hand and led him toward the hotel entrance. Standing on tip-toes she wrapped her arms around his neck and whispered in his ear. "Be careful out there tonight."

"I will." He nibbled playfully on her ear lobe. "Keep a good eye on those two. I've heard rumors about her. Supposedly she can lift an automobile over her head without even trying."

"She told me she came from the arctic." Sue shivered in his arms.

"Pure science fiction." Stephen smiled. "Don't forget, keep them busy tomorrow."

"Remember to be careful." She pulled his face toward her and kissed him roughly on the lips.

"You're not making it easy to leave." He said ending the embrace.

A feeling of dread settled in her stomach, as Sue walked toward the waiting elevator. She wanted Stephen to stay off the streets, to abandon his alter ego. She knew better. The Moon Man would continue to prowl the dark corners of Great City, fighting to drive the criminals and vermin away.

"He's not going to get much sleep," Blake mumbled, stepping inside the waiting elevator.

"Miss McEwen, how are you this evening?" the operator asked.

"I'm fine, Jake." She turned to Blake and Amazona. "He never gets enough sleep. I expect he'll make a circle through town, just to make sure everything is quiet before he goes home."

The doors closed slowly. The box jerked upward. The hand above the doors counted off the floors. At the sixth it dinged to a stop, the attendant unlocked and opened the doors. "Your guests are just down the hall, Miss McEwen, room 607."

"Thank you, Jake." Sue turned to Blake and Amazona, a frown crinkled her face. "You only have one room?"

"One room is all we need." A puzzled look wrinkled the mighty woman's face.

"Keep it to yourself that the two of you aren't married." Sue walked them to their room. "That behavior may be alright in California, but it's frowned on in Great City."

"We'll keep it under our hat." Blake paused at the door.

Sue turned and walked down the hall to her door.

"I'm going out tonight," Amazona mumbled. "I might get lucky and find the Moon Man."

"That's a bad idea." Blake fitted the key in the lock and gave it a twist.

"Besides, you don't know the city. What if you get lost?"

"Then, I'll ask for directions." Amazona smiled. "I'm a big girl. I can take care of myself."

"No doubt of that, but when the good citizens get a look of you in that unitard, you'll stop city traffic."

A blush crept up her face. "I'll be back before daylight."

Sue lingered in the hallway, listening to the couple's muted conversation.

Stephen stifled a yawn as he drove the Roadster through the northeast section of town. Great City seemed unusually quiet. Even the local gin joints had closed up for the night. He spied Johnny Bowlegs, a Great War vet staggering down the sidewalk. He had served with the AEF cavalry, under General Black Jack Pershing. The old man had fallen on hard times. He'd lost everything during the depression and lacked the will to fight to get it back.

The detective-sergeant pulled to the curb. "Hey, Johnny, Johnny Bowlegs, you need a ride?"

The old man spun at the familiar voice and nearly fell. He closed one eye and squinted with the other. "Steve, is that you?" He staggered to the automobile. "Boy am I glad to see you, I wasn't looking forward to walking back to my crib."

"Nate Wilkerson closed up early tonight. The whole town is quiet." Johnny crawled into the passenger seat. Stephen pulled away from the curb and sped down the deserted roadway. "At least, the night officers will get a peaceful shift."

"For a little while." Johnny nodded. "I heard some goons talking. They was speaking German, didn't think I understood, but I picked up a fair share of the lingo when I was overseas."

"What did they say?" Stephen demanded.

"They're planning a big heist down at the hub, they think they're gonna hit a big score. You can feel it in the air. Something big is gonna happen tonight."

"Anything else?" Stephen stared at the old man. "Come on, Johnny, did they say anything else?"

"The Moon Man," Johnny slurred. "They've got a trap set for him. They want him to show up; they want to kill him bad. He nailed some of their buddies, when he burned the Rosenfeld Market."

Stephen glanced along the side streets. "Your place is just ahead." He parked along the trash filled gutter. "Do yourself a favor, Johnny. Stay home for the rest of the night."

The old drunk nodded, waving his finger at Stephen. "One more thing, Steve. This guy came in, tall fellah, talked through his nose. When he got there, those krauts clammed up and followed him outside. After that, Nate ran everybody outside."

"Thanks, Johnny. Take care of yourself." A wreath of smoke rose from the tailpipe, as Stephen accelerated down the road.

He parked the roadster a half mile from the railway depot and the switch yard. He glanced up and down the deserted roadway. *Never seen the streets this empty.* He pulled the dark soft leather gloves on his hands and removed his cloak and the cracked Argus glass helmet from the trunk. He checked his pistol and grabbed two loaded magazines.

Steve shoved the pistol in his interior coat pocket. The sound of voices drifted through the night. *They're close.* He slipped the cloak over his shoulders and tied it fast. The round shiny globe swallowed his head. He reached behind his head and locked it into place with a special clasp at the back of his neck.

The Moon Man ran forward, keeping to the shadows, taking care to remain within hearing distance of the group ahead. He closed the distance and picked up a few words of the conversation.

"You guys go down to the..." the nasally voice faded. "The safe's in the wheel house"

That's Slingshot McGuire. The Moon Man's grip tightened on the pistol. He didn't keep the promise he'd made to Angel earlier. He was determined to succeed this time.

Wish I knew what they're after. He quickened his pace. A large group of men left the safety of the shadows and crossed under a lone streetlight into the railway yard.

The large man gestured wildly, the men behind him split into three groups. From his position Slingshot's voice sounded like a loud bee drone. The Moon Man waited as the crooks disappeared from sight. Satisfied they were far enough ahead; he dashed across the street and slipped through a huge gap in the fence.

A bullet splattered at his feet. The Moon Man leaped for safety. He triggered a quick off-balance shot with the .45 and dove behind a line of crates waiting to be loaded on the transports. A railcar burned at the far end of the line. Red flames danced into the sky, coloring the sparse clouds.

"Over here, the Moon Man is behind those crates."

Bullets smacked the wooden containers, passing through to the other side. The Moon Man belly crawled down the line of shipping boxes. A hail of bullets slapped the planks and passed over his head. Wood splinters rained down on his shoulders and bounced from the glass helmet.

"You can't escape, Moon Man." A sultry female voice reached his ears. "I have men circling your position. We'll have you in a cross fire."

Keep talking, just keep talking. A narrow space between two crates offered him a measure of protection and a safe space to fire on his attackers. "You're the Veiled Lady. What are you doing in Great City? I thought Detroit was your turf."

Her jubilant laugh caught on the night breeze. "I go where I'm needed, and I'm needed in Great City. From your reputation, I expected more from you. You sure wouldn't cut the mustard in Detroit."

"Don't count me out yet." He reached the niche in the line of containers, rising to a crouch. His attackers stood thirty feet away, looking in the other direction. His eyes centered on the tall woman, wearing an expensive evening dress slit to mid-thigh, a white veil concealed her face.

"Think I'll hang your corpse at city hall. That kind of visual aide will really pull this operation together." She turned to her henchmen. "Kill him."

The Moon Man sighted down the barrel, lining his first shot on the Veiled Lady's ample bosom. His finger squeezed the trigger.

Amazona stepped from the bathroom. The unitard fit her like a glove. "I'm off to see the town."

"Be careful in that thing, I don't know if the locals can handle you in that outfit," Blake joked. His smiling face hardened, a serious glint entered his eyes. "Does it bother you, that we're not married?"

"Sue didn't mean anything with her remark. I expect our living arrangement would shock several people, if it were common knowledge." Amazona raised the window and peered at her surroundings. "There's a drain pipe here. I'll use it to climb down."

"Remember, you're not bullet proof. Just give the town the once over. Don't get into any scrapes." He stood in the center of the room, hands perched on his hips.

"You can't escape, Moon Man. We'll have you in a cross fire."

"Don't worry about me." She crossed the space between them and planted a long lasting kiss on Blake's lips. She smiled and returned to the window and shimmied down the drainpipe.

In seconds her feet touched the concrete sidewalk. Amazona glanced up and down the near-deserted street. A line of headlights approached from the south, she watched as they sped past. The driver and a single woman occupied the lead vehicle.

"The Veiled Lady." She mumbled stepping into the alley. Hard desperate faces glanced from the windows of the pursuit vehicles. "They're moving with a purpose." She jogged down the sidewalk, following the diminishing taillights.

"Hey, beautiful, where have you been all my life?" A young man approached her from behind. "Does your mama know you're out trolling the town?"

"Go away, leave me alone." Amazona answered defiantly, the harsh scent of alcohol filled her nostrils. She walked past the Friendship Hall and noticed two police officers asleep in the black and white cruiser.

"Are there more like you at home?" The young man drew closer, reaching out for her arm.

"I am the last female of my kind. I am Amazona, the mighty woman." Her cold stare fastened on the man. "Now stop following me."

"You've got some great legs, almost as nice as Betty Grable's, but you've got a bigger set than she has."

Amazona turned on the startled man. Her hand fisted in his shirt, and lifted him from the ground. "In my land, men do not accost women so freely. If you care for your well-being, leave me alone."

The hood gulped and nodded. "Sure Doll, anything you say."

The sound of gunfire drifted through the still night. "You were trying to divert me from my destination. Crawl back to your masters and tell them you failed." She ran to the sounds of battle. Long legs moved with the grace and beauty of a jungle cat. Soft-soled cloth shoes slapped the concrete as she closed the distance swiftly.

Leaping flames colored the southern sky. Hot embers rained down on Amazona's head. The echo of gunfire intensified. She peered from the darkness at the mayhem ahead. A strangely dressed man wearing a black cloak and a fishbowl on his head rose from a row of wooden shipping crates. Death-dealing lead flew from the pistol in his hand.

"So, that's the Moon Man." Amazona ran into the midst of the firefight.

"What the hell?" a voice shouted with a nasally twang. "Who in the hell is the dame?"

"I don't know, but my God, look at those legs."

Bullets whizzed past her head, catching her dark hair in the artificial breeze. Amazona ducked behind a large crate, crushing the wooden shell under her fingers. Muscles bunched in her arm and back, as she lifted the heavy container effortlessly above her head.

"Look at that? I've never seen anyone that strong."

"Quit staring; put a bullet in that witch." A nasally voice shouted.

The crate smashed into the center of the hoodlums with a tremendous crash and a rain of splintered wood. A bullet burned her arm, as she moved to the next container.

The Moon Man took advantage of the diversion. His finger squeezed the trigger twice in rapid succession. A broad hood turned to run. The bullets caught him, as he stepped in front of The Veiled Lady, saving her life. The masked man ejected the spent magazine, and jammed the second into the butt of the automatic. Gun blazing, he climbed atop a smaller crate. His automatic rained hot lead on the scattering thugs.

"Kill them both." The Veiled Lady turned and ran from the gun battle.

Slingshot McGuire dodged a hail of bullets and sprinted to the nearest boxcar. He ducked behind the steel wheels. His gang scattered like rats on a sinking ship.

A tolling bell echoed from the buildings. The ear-splitting screech of a siren followed soon after. The Moon Man's mask reflected the bright red flames, as he jumped to the ground.

"I don't know what your game is, but the police are very anxious to speak to you." Amazona rounded the crates, her hands clenched into fists.

The Moon Man took a wary step backward. "I don't have a quarrel with you. Out of my way, I have business to attend to. Great City is under my protection."

"Protection?" Amazona shook her head. "You're no better than the vermin crawling in the gutters."

"I don't want to fight you. I have a job to finish. Those criminals are tied in with the Nazis, and I'm going to stop them." He turned to leave.

A crate landed in front of him, the wooden sides exploded outward showering him with a variety of metal bolts. The Moon Man spun, the .45 gripped in his fist.

Amazona dashed forward. Her hands circled the masked man's wrists and squeezed. The automatic dropped from his numb hand. "You're not going anywhere."

He kicked the outside of her right knee with all his strength. Amazona'a grip eased. The Moon Man yanked one hand free and drove a hard elbow into the point of her jaw. The vicious unexpected blow dropped her to her knees.

The Moon Man's tingling hand closed on the pistol and jammed it in his pocket. Flashing lights appeared in the distance. He knew the fire department and police would arrive within minutes. The masked man turned and ran into the darkness.

"I won't be stopped that easily." She jumped to her feet and raced after the fleeing figure.

Feeling slowly returned to his numb hand. Hot breath mixed with the sweat streaming down his face. A column of steam passed his face escaping through the hole near his eye. He raced past the flaming boxcar, hoping the heat would slow his determined pursuer.

"You're only delaying the inevitable."

Fear gnawed at the Moon Man. He couldn't be caught. He couldn't be unmasked as Stephen Thatcher and spend the rest of his life in prison. The shame would destroy Sue and ruin Gil and his father's careers. In desperation, he circled an aged *Plymouth* parked in the shadows.

The mighty woman reached out. Metal shrieked, as her fingers sank into the smooth finish. Muscles strained and sinew bunched, with a single jerk, she lifted the vehicle over her head.

"This is an act of desperation. You can't escape me." Her teeth gritted together, shoulders quivering. Metal crumpled beneath her grip. She tossed the vehicle in the air like a toy. It crashed to the highway, the windows exploded outward.

A movement in the darkness caught the Moon Man's eyes. Straining to see through the interior fog, he drew the .45 from his pocket. "Behind you."

"That old trick won't work with me."

Slingshot McGuire stepped into the light. His face creased in a rodent smile. He leveled the automatic at the mighty woman's back. His finger slowly tightened on the trigger.

"You lack the courage to fight me unarmed," Amazona taunted. "I could have thrown that car on your head, but I choose to fight with honor."

The gun bucked in the Moon Man's hand. A tendril of smoke rose from the barrel. Slingshot McGuire bent in the middle, a muffled groan escaped his lips. The .45 dropped from his hand and clattered to the sidewalk.

Amazona stared in amazement. Her eyes bulged to the size of silver dollars. She looked behind her at the prone body and the pistol lying near McGuire's outstretched hand. "You weren't shooting at me."

"Great City and its people are under my protection. That includes you."

He jammed the pistol in his pocket. "I fight for the people that can't fight for themselves." The squalling siren grew louder, colored lights reflected from the Argus glass helmet. The cloak flapped in the air, as he turned and raced into the night.

The police cruiser screeched to a stop. A befuddled uniformed officer jumped from the vehicle, .38 gripped tightly in his fist. "What the hell is going on here?"

"I'm very unhappy." Madame Terror stared at the Veiled Lady. Fritz Kuhn stood by her side, his face pale and drawn. "The trains are not destroyed, Moon Man escaped. We must control the area, prevent any troops from arriving."

"Calm down." She lifted the bottom half of her veil showing smooth skin and a firm chin. A long-stemmed wine glass slipped under the covering, she sipped the scarlet liquid. "My men will mix with the workmen; we'll control the telegraph and telephones. The rest will deal with the Moon Man, start landing your own troops tomorrow night."

"We can't allow any American troops access to Great City, until we are in control," Kuhn said.

"Everything is under control. If any troops come in by rail, we'll kill them before they can leave the passenger cars." She placed the glass on the table to her right. "Nice vintage, twenty-seven merlot, I believe." The Veiled Lady crossed her legs, giving Kuhn a nice view of her thighs. "We'll control this town in two days."

Kuhn stared at the stockings and the hint of a garter, a lecherous smile on his face. "We have fifty men now. Others are waiting in a tanker off shore. When the moment is right, they'll leave the ship in small speedboats to assist our soldiers in subjugating the city."

"If you fail, you'll both die slowly." Madame Terror rose to her feet. She turned and departed into the darkness.

"Nice boss you've got there." The Veiled Lady straightened her dress and climbed to her feet. "Have my money ready when this is over. There's a nice estate in South America I'd like to purchase."

"He saved your life?" Blake sipped at his coffee, staring across at the ebony-haired beauty on the far side of the table. Her trademark red unitard soot stained and torn. "Maybe he's not the bad egg the local papers make him out to be."

"He claimed to be the city's protector." Amazona shrugged. "Maybe he is." She spotted a small slip of paper wedged under the second coffee cup on the tray and tugged it free. "What's this?"

"Might be a note from one of your admirers"

Amazona unfolded the note. "It is." She passed the message to Blake. "It's from the Moon Man."

Blake stared at the cryptic scrawl. "Glad you made it home safely. Tell your boyfriend not to trust Kuhn. Meet me, Henderson's Trucking, Midnight." He shook his head slowly. "Can't say much for his art work." The moon he drew in the corner looks like a baseball. Are you going?"

"After I get some sleep. I'll walk around the city and get my bearings." Amazona yawned.

"Get some shut-eye." Blake finished his coffee. "I'm going to impose on Sue to show me the city and drive me to the Friendship Hall." He rose from the table, grabbed a light jacket and headed for the door.

The door swung open easily under his hand, revealing Sue McEwen on the other side. "I was just thinking about you." He smiled. "Come in, would you like some coffee?"

"No, I was on my way down town." Her eyes fastened on Amazona lounging at the small table. A blush crept up her face. "I thought I'd give the two of you a guided tour of the city."

"Thanks." Amazona nodded. "But I'm going to sleep." She rose to her feet.

Sue noticed her torn, stained costume. "Goodness, what happened to you?"

"Zona, went for a late night walk to the rail yard." Blake stepped into the hallway. "Someone tried to burn the place down."

"Really," Sue gasped. "Are you hurt?"

Amazona shook her head, dark hair flaring around her shoulders.

"Zona's a tough girl." He closed the door behind him. "Now, what were you saying about a tour of the town?"

"Come on, I know all the local landmarks."

They walked down the hallway, side by side, unaware of the close set eyes watching them from an open door down the hallway.

"What's the matter with you?" Gil McEwen demanded. "Didn't you get any sleep last night?"

"No, couldn't shut my mind down, after I delivered our guests to the hotel." Stephen stifled a yawn. "I was awake when the fire started at the train yard, drove over to see if I could help."

"Yeah, some of the uniforms told me you were there." Gil stared at the line of workmen passing through the large doors of the Friendship Hall. "You should keep your mind on our assignment."

"Gil, they were a wild mob." Stephen ran a hand through his unruly hair. "They burned two freight cars and part of the loading bay."

"And the Moon Man killed four people." Gil shook his head. "One day I'll catch that man. I'm gonna rip that fishbowl off his head and smash it at his feet."

"We don't know the Moon Man was there." Stephen stepped forward, gazing into the older man's eyes. "I talked to the firemen and the uniforms. No one saw him."

"I know he was there, I've got a feeling in my gut."

"Hey, there's Sue." Stephen pointed at a red convertible pulling to the curb. "I asked her to drive Manners and Amazona around today, show them the sights and drop him off here."

"Guy has a big reputation in California, and that girl of his is some looker." Gil turned toward the street to see his daughter and Blake Manners step to the sidewalk.

Sue scampered forward and threw herself into Stephen's arms, planting a forceful kiss on his lips. "Amazona's still at the hotel." She pulled away slowly, whispering in his ear. "Her outfit was torn and smoke blackened."

"Keep Manners busy. I don't want him coming back here till this afternoon."

"Come on you two, wait until you're married." Gil slapped Stephen's shoulder. "You're ignoring your guest, Sue."

"I'm so sorry." Sue stepped back staring at the sidewalk. "I can't help myself sometimes."

"I know the feeling. I don't understand what Zona sees in me, but I'm fortunate to have her." Blake turned to the large building. "So that's the Friendship Hall." He shook his head. "I don't see the Nazis as a friendly bunch."

"Amen." Gil nodded. "I'd like to run these bums out of town."

"Dad," Sue scolded. "You know the mayor is counting on the extra income to keep Great City solvent."

"She's right." Stephen nodded. "This may be the difference in hiring more cops or sending people home."

"I still don't like it. It's like putting the fox in the hen house."

"Come on." Sue caught the reporter's arm. "Let's see the town then we'll come back here."

"I can't say no to a pretty girl." Blake walked her to the roadster. "As long as I can get an interview with Kuhn, I'm sitting pretty."

Two men moved silently down the hallway. A thin sharp nosed rat-faced man paused at the door, pulling a lock-pick kit from his ill-fitting suit.

"Come on, Charlie. Get that damned door open." His companion, a burly man with a large brow ridge, stared down the hallway. His hand shoved deep in his coat pocket. "The boss ain't gonna like it, if we keep her waiting."

"Shut yer gob, Dave," Rat-face whispered. "I'm moving as fast as I can. Why does the boss want this dame?"

"She was at the relay station last night. This babe is strong. I ain't ever seen anyone this stout. A circus strong man would turn green with envy." Dave's close set eyes focused on the elevator. "Hurry up."

The lock clicked open. "There, now get in there and do your stuff." He gave the door a gentle shove. It swung open on well-oiled hinges.

Dave quietly stepped inside; a filthy torn unitard draped over the sofa caught his attention. Deep wrinkles creased his forehead, his heavy brow lifted. He eased the .38 snub-nose from his jacket.

"Blake is that you?" A sultry voice came from the bathroom. "I'm taking a bath. I'll be out in a few minutes."

Dave froze in position.

"You're back early. How did the interview with Kuhn go?"

Charlie crept to Dave's side. The smaller of the two he moved across the floor without making a sound, taking a position near the closed door.

"Blake, answer me." The sound of dripping water filled the room. The door opened slowly. A wet towel wrapped figure stood framed in the threshold, a bar of soap in her hand. "You're not Blake."

"No, toots, I ain't Blake." A lecherous gap-toothed smile split Dave's face. "Get some clothes on, someone wants to see you."

"I see." Amazona hurled the soap with all her strength. The bar smacked the hood between the eyes.

Dave collapsed to the floor, wide eyes staring at the ceiling.

Amazona rushed forward, the towel fell from her body. Her hand fisted in Dave's shirt yanking him to his feet. "Who are you working for?" She shook him roughly. His head bobbed back and forth on his shoulders. "Who sent you?"

Cold steel settled at the base of her skull. "You've got a great body, Sister, but if you make another move without my okay, I'll blow your brains out."

She let the half-conscious hood fall to the floor. "What's your game?" Her fisted hands settled on her hips.

"The boss wants to see you. Get some clothes on. You're going on a short trip." Charlie motioned with the pistol. "I saw what you did last night. You're strong, but I see a slug nicked your arm so you're not bullet proof. You make a move I don't like and I'll empty this roscoe. You got that?

Amazona nodded. "Turn your back while I dress."

"You've got to be kidding sister. I've seen everything you've got. So don't be bashful." Charlie aimed the pistol at her head. "Now move or I'll kill you where you stand."

"What happened?" Dave managed to sit up, massaging an egg sized knot on his forehead.

"The beauty laid you out cold." Charlie let out a rat squeak laugh. "Lucky for us she didn't pick up your rod or she might have killed us both." He turned to Amazona. "Get some clothes on."

Fifteen minutes later they stepped through the hotel door to the sidewalk. "Okay, Sister, third car down on the right. Dave's gonna get in first, and you're gonna sit right next to him. I'm sitting on your other side. You'll have two guns in your ribs all the time. Try anything at all and we'll blow you in half." He nudged her in the side with the pistol. "You understand?"

"Yes, I understand." Her hand rested on the *Packard's* door handle. Dave crossed to the far side and settled into the rear seat.

"Get in." Charlie jammed the cold steel against her spine.

She opened the door and scooted to the center, Charlie followed her inside. The pistol barrel gouged her flesh through the blue dress. "Let's roll," Charlie said.

The driver nodded. He slipped the heavy car into gear and pulled into traffic.

"Where are we going?" Amazona squirmed away from the automatic pressing her ribs.

"You'll find out, Toots."

Sue parked the Ford near the curb. She and Blake had completed the tour of the city and ate lunch at Pierre's, a fashionable restaurant on the east side. She waved to Stephen and her father.

"I want some good pictures." He patted the new camera sitting on the seat between them. "This beauty should do the trick. That camera shop you recommended certainly has up to date merchandise."

"Alex prides himself on carrying the best products." She stepped to the sidewalk. "I really want to get a good look at the decorations inside."

"You two be careful in there." Gil walked up slowly and hugged his daughter close. "I've got to go downtown, the chief wants a word."

"We'll be fine, Dad." She planted a kiss on his cheek.

"Is Fritz Kuhn inside?" Blake lifted the camera from the rear seat.

"Haven't seen him today. Check with Steve when you're finished." Gil nodded. "I don't trust those guys in there."

"Will do." Sue threw a mock salute.

"Don't worry, Gil. The Nazis won't try anything here. Timing's not right." Blake and Sue slowly mounted the stairs leading to the massive front door.

A short fussy man met them at the entrance. "Please come in, I am Airbert Wallisch. I will be your guide." He rubbed his hands together; a circle of sweat beaded his forehead.

"Where's Fritz Kuhn?" Blake shook the nervous man's hand. "I wanted to interview him for my newspaper."

"Yes, yes, I know." Wallisch scarped his beefy jowls. "He was called away to Massachusetts. I'm very sorry. I'll answer any questions you have." He turned and led them inside.

"What about Kuhn? Will he be back for the rally?" Sue asked.

"Uh," Wallisch licked his lips. "No, unfortunately he won't be able to attend. Please come this way." He led them into the bowels of the Friendship Hall, he stopped before the wide auditorium.

"Something's wrong," Sue whispered to Blake.

"You've got that right," a gravelly voice whispered behind her. "Just keep walking."

"What's going on here?" Blake stopped. A gun barrel settled between his shoulders and prodded him forward.

"The boss wants to talk to you. Don't worry your squeeze is waiting for you. We snatched her earlier."

"Get them out of here, quietly." Wallisch wiped sweat from his forehead.

"Relax, Little Man, the boss will handle things. Just make sure the rally kicks off on time." A ham sized hand closed on Blake's shoulder. "Keep moving, we're going out the back way, and don't make any sudden moves or you'll never walk again."

"My father is Lieutenant Gil McEwen. If you harm me he'll hunt all of you down." Sue turned and stared up at a tall burly man.

"Shut-up and get moving." He backhanded her across the mouth. "No more of your lip, I don't care who your daddy is."

Tears formed in Sue's eyes. She pulled a handkerchief from her purse wiped a line of blood from her split-lip. Her small hands closed into fists.

"Come on, Sue." Blake grabbed her sleeve and tugged her along. "We'll get our turn later."

"Keep dreaming, Fellah, keep dreaming." The hood shoved them through a rear door into the alley to a waiting sedan. "Get in the car and keep your mouth shut."

"Whatever you say." Blake nodded.

The handkerchief dropped from Sue's hand, as she crawled into the back seat.

Stephen tugged his pocket watch from his vest. *Blake must be getting a great story. They've been inside for nearly two hours.* A frown creased his face. *Think I'll check on them.* He approached the huge oak door. His hand closed on the knob and found it locked.

"What's going on?" His clenched fist pounded on a hardwood panel. "Open up in there," he shouted. "Great City Police Department."

The door cracked open. A single eye gazed from the slit. "What do you want? I'm very busy."

"Detective-Sergeant Stephen Thatcher." He pulled his badge from his pocket and held it close to the staring orb. "I need to come inside and look around."

"We're very busy. We're arranging the portraits and flowers now. Please come back later." A line of sweat threaded down his forehead and circled the wide eye. "I won't have you interfering with the workmen."

"What workmen? Your crew went home an hour ago. Open up, I just want a quick look around." Stephen's hand slipped into his pocket, circling the grip of his back-up snub-nose .38. "I'm looking for the reporter and the young lady that came in a little while ago."

"You must be mistaken, Officer. Reporters aren't allowed inside a Bund rally." He moved to shut the door.

Stephen palm slammed the door above the knob. The edge of the hardwood cracked the small nervous man in the forehead. He fell backwards landing on his butt.

"How dare you attack me?" The small man blustered. Blood flowed around his eye, mixing with the sweat, and dripped from his beefy jowls. "I'll report you to the Chief of Police and the Mayor."

Stephen yanked the pistol free and thumb cocked the hammer. He pressed the barrel to Wallisch's forehead. "You've got ten seconds to tell me where the girl and the reporter went or I'll blow your head off."

The nervous man's eyes focused on the curled trigger finger. His mouth dropped as it slowly tightened. "Wait," He swallowed. "Don't kill me, please."

"Where are they?"

"Please I don't know. I was only Kuhn's assistant. I don't know anything about the operation." The short man's lower jaw quivered.

"Who took them?" The pressure from the pistol barrel increased. "How did they get them out of here?"

"The Veiled Lady's men took them out the back," he stammered.

Stephen removed the pistol from the frightened man's forehead, leaving a white ring on the German's flesh. "Which one?"

"I don't know his name. He's a big guy. Talks funny, like he has a mouth full of gravel." Wallisch slowly climbed to his feet.

"Sounds like Buddy Malone." Stephen grabbed Wallisch by the collar and pushed him toward the rear exit. "When did Kuhn hire the Veiled Lady?"

The man stumbled over his own feet. "He didn't hire her. The woman from Japan brought her in on this operation."

"A Japanese woman," Stephen whispered. "Does she have a name?"

"Madame Terror. Kuhn called her Madame Terror." Wallisch stopped at the door, unwilling to grasp the knob.

"I need to come inside and look around."

Stephen reached around his rotund belly and twisted the brass fixture. He shoved Wallisch through the opening. The Nazi sympathizer fell to his knees in the alley. His eyes fastened on the bloodstained white lace hanky. He reached out attempting to grab it.

Stephen stepped on the back of the Nazi's hand, grinding the sole of his shoe into his flesh. "What's this?" He snatched it from Wallisch's fingers. His eyes widened, a crimson flush colored his neck and crawled up his face, as his eyes settled on the red stain.

"I want the truth." Stephen stuffed the hanky in his pocket. "You know where they are. The only way you're gonna see tomorrow is to tell me what I want to know."

Prodding guns forced Blake and Sue inside the empty Wilson Processing Plant. Sue glanced around the interior and noticed a single shoe mixed with the trash and debris scattered across the floor.

"Keep moving, Doll." The coarse voiced thug shoved her forward. "You ain't here to admire the decor."

Sue turned and glared at the huge brute, but kept control of her tongue.

"Where's Zona?" Blake demanded. "What have you done with her?"

"Your girlfriend's safe, Manners, for the moment at least." A woman in a white dress, wearing a black hat and veil, appeared at the far side of the room. She gripped a small caliber automatic in her fist. "I've asked her several questions, but she refused to answer me." She turned to her brooding hireling. "Take them to the back. We'll have a party." Her lilting laughter drifted to the ceiling.

Blake and Sue walked through an ancient freezer door into a huge thick walled room. "This is the cold room." The Veiled Lady's musical voice rang from the walls. "Twenty years ago this place would be filled with crates of fish and ice. The walls are insulated and nearly three feet thick. They make an excellent sound barrier."

A tall proud woman with dark hair, her bound hands stretched above her head met Blake's eyes. "Amazona." He rushed forward, a mallet-like fist struck him in the back of the head. He pitched forward, breaking his fall at the last instant. "What did you do to her?"

"Blake, I'm sorry they caught you." Blood trickled from her left nostril, pooling around her lips.

"Be Quiet, no talking." A woman, struggling with the English language, sat in the shadows. "Why are you here?"

"What are you talking about?" Blake gazed at the dark figure. "I work for the Daily Sun in San Francisco. I'm here to do a story on the German-American Bund."

"You Lie. Why are you here?" The voice rose to a screech.

The Veiled Lady stepped between Blake and Amazona. "You have to forgive Madame Terror. English isn't her native tongue. Germany and Japan have invested a great amount of time and a considerable amount of money in this operation. I'm going to ask you several questions. If you refuse to answer or lie to me, one of you will be punished."

"Who do you work for?" She asked. "Why are you here?"

"I'm here to get a story. I work for the Daily Sun," Blake repeated.

"I guess you need a demonstration." The Veiled Lady moved to Amazona's side. She moved the slit on her dress to the side and removed a long glass tube from her garter and held it up for Blake to see. "This is a shock tube, a nasty little device the Nazis dreamed up."

She touched it to Amazona's bare shoulder. A yellow arc traveled from two small points to the Mighty Woman's flesh. Blue smoke rose from her charred skin. Amazona arched her back in agony. A muted scream escaped her clenched lips.

"Don't hurt her," Blake screamed. "I'll tell you everything."

The roadster slid around the turn, leaning on the outer wheels for a brief instant, before it settled back to the roadway. Stephen shifted to a higher gear and popped the clutch. The light car circled the vehicle on the right, much to the chagrin of the other driver, and hurtled down the road.

After several minutes of intense questioning, Wallisch had spilled the beans. The Bund Rally was a sham, an excuse to bring Nazi soldiers into Great City. They tried to burn the rail yard to prevent any possible aid from reaching Great City. At midnight, the troops would attack Police headquarters. One hundred hand-selected storm-troopers would land at the docks and move toward the center of the city. If their plan succeeded, Great City would be under Nazi control within hours.

Stephen gnawed his bottom lip. According to Wallisch, the Nazis had taken Sue, Blake and Amazona to an old abandoned fishery near the waterfront. They knew the reporter had connections with the FBI and assumed he and the Mighty Woman were sent to the city to stop them.

He left Wallisch handcuffed to a light pole in front of the Friendship Hall. He used the interior phone to call the station. He missed Gil, but spoke to his father and gave him all the information.

Stephen pressed the gas pedal to the floor. He had to rescue Sue and the others and stop the Nazis from getting a foothold in the city. He glanced in the rearview mirror. A sedan circled the corner, smoke belched from the tailpipe as it rushed forward.

He held the wheel with one hand and tugged the .45 free with the other. Next he pulled the .38 backup pistol from his coat and laid it on the seat beside him. A steely glint settled in his eyes; if those were Madame Terror's men he'd be ready.

The docks lay six blocks ahead, and the trailing vehicle was right on his bumper. A thin rat-faced man leaned from the window, a Tommy-gun cradled in his arms. His eyes glowed with maniacal glee, as he pulled the trigger.

The back windshield shattered, shards of glass filled the seat and pelted the back of his head. Stephen hit the brakes and twisted the wheel savagely to the left. The roadster pivoted in a boil of smoke. He lifted the .38 and fired at the shooter.

Rat-face crumbled, the Tommy-gun fell from his lifeless hands the body dropped from the window and slid across the abrasive road, leaving bits of flesh in his wake. The sedan sped past on its way to the docks. Stephen fought to control the roadster. The car jumped the curb, the front bumper smashed into a light pole. Stephen's head slammed the steering wheel.

Blood streamed from his forehead. Clumsy hands pawed at the handle, before he managed to open the door. Stephen stumbled to the highway, dizzy and confused. *Wilson's Processing, I've got to get to Wilson's Processing.* He pushed himself to his feet. A stabbing pain shot through his right leg.

He felt along the thigh and found a sliver of glass embedded in the flesh above the knee. Stephen gritted his teeth and pulled it free. The rush of pain banished the wooziness from his brain. Gathering his pistols from the front seat and floorboard, he unlocked the trunk and retrieved the cloak and the Argus mask with the broken chip near the eye.

The last rays of the dying sun painted the sky a dark red cast. *I've got to find Sue.* Pain lanced through his leg, as he trotted toward the processing plant. He knew the place would be swarming with armed men, ready and willing to gun him down in their attempt to control the city. Stephen pushed the pain from his mind. His pace gradually increased, as he worked the stiffness from his muscles.

He stood in the shadows outside the processing plant thirty minutes later. His roving eyes spotted the sedan parked beyond the security fence. Guards stood outside in the deep shadows and lounged at every window.

"I've got to find a way inside." As he watched, six men ran from the rundown building and piled into the sedan. The vehicle sped through the gate, smoke boiling from the rear tires. "They're going to the docks to welcome the troops and take control of the waterway."

A loud scream echoed from the white block building, the guards rushed from their post toward the ruckus coming from the bowels of the fishery. "That's my cue." Stephen flipped the dark cloak over his shoulders and slipped the Argus glass bowl over his head, locking it into place. Armed with both pistols he charged the open gate of the make-shift fortress.

"Stop her!" Madame Terror shouted.

Tendons stood out along Amazona's arms, with a single jerk the multiple strands of rope popped like a gunshot. With the grace and speed of a panther, she turned, her hands fisted in the collars of the two hoods within reach. She lifted them from the floor and threw them across the room. They slammed the concrete wall with a resounding thud.

A hurried gunshot splattered the floor. Concrete chips pelted her legs. She leaped toward the shooter. A rock hard fist smashed his jaw to bony splinters. He collapsed to the floor out of the fight. Amazona ran toward the three men holding Blake and Sue.

A hulking thug centered his .45 on her chest. Amazona watched in horror, as his finger tightened on the trigger. A gun blast echoed from the walls, blood sprayed Blake and Sue. The hoods mouth stretched open in a wide 0, the pistol clattered to the floor as he toppled. The Moon Man stepped into the light, smoke curled from the barrel of his .45.

"Moon Man, look out," Sue screamed. She stamped on a gunman's foot, grinding her high heel into his instep.

Thunder filled the room. Hot lead spit from the Moon Man's automatic. The two men collapsed to the floor, red dots stained their chests. Bullets buzzed past the glass helmet and tugged at his cloak.

"Get out of here," he shouted. Cocking the hammer on the .38, he nailed a burly man running into the large room. The thug's finger closed on the trigger, .45 slugs bounced from the walls and peppered the ceiling. "Get to the docks. German soldiers are going to land, if they can get a foothold in Great City, they'll ship in more troops and attack the United States from within." Amazona grabbed the ropes binding Blake and Sue and snapped them like string.

Sue snatched a Tommy-gun from the floor. She glanced toward Blake. The reporter mimicked her movements. "Amazona grab a weapon. We've got to get to the docks and stop those krauts."

She shook her head. "I don't use weapons. My strength will be enough."

"Your strength can't stop a bullet." Sue ran for the door, the rifle gripped tightly in her hands. "Come on, follow me." She disappeared into the night. The others followed on her heels.

Madame Terror jumped from her chair. An oriental fan covered her features as she bolted for safety through a side door.

"Damn you! Damn you, why did you interfere?" the Veiled lady screamed. She yanked a small caliber weapon from her stockings and triggered three quick shots at the Moon Man.

Two sailed wide; the third burned the flesh along his ribs. The .38 dropped from his hand and vanished in the debris. The Moon Man held his elbow close to his ribcage, using the coat sleeve to staunch the flow of blood. He triggered two quick shots at the Veiled Lady. The woman turned and followed the oriental woman to safety.

A bullet tugged at his pant leg. The Moon Man dove for cover, as a Tommy-gun showered his position. Lead slugs whistled past his head and splattered a scrap pile of lumber.

"Look," Sue panted. Holding her aching sides, she pointed out into the bay. The headlights of two small boats cut through the darkness headed toward shore. "That must be the Germans."

"We don't know that." Amazona shook her head. "You can't fire. There could be innocents aboard those boats."

Bullets smacked the wall behind them and careened through the air. "I don't think there's any doubt now." Sue dropped to the rough-hewn boards. The heavy rifle settled into her shoulder. Sighting down the barrel, she squeezed the trigger. The stock slammed her shoulder, the wide shots spraying the water.

"You're not hitting anything." Blake raised the weapon, and fired on the approaching lights. Answering fire smacked the dock. Wood chips filled the air. "Fire at the boats; we have to keep them from landing"

Sue shifted the rifle and aimed at the closing boats. "If we can make it hot enough for them they won't try to land." She failed to see the figure in the shadows.

"Hold them off." Amazona rose to her feet. She kicked the low-heeled shoes from her feet. "I'll circle behind the others." She raced forward and dove into the water.

"I hope she knows what she's doing? That water's cold this time of year," Sue shouted.

A smile touched Blake's face. "Don't worry about Zona. She's used to the cold."

Amazona held her breath, gliding through the water like a porpoise. She emerged when she calculated she'd traveled an appropriate distance. Her fingers sank into the rough surface of one of the docks numerous supports, water streamed from her hair and clothes, as she pulled herself from the water's frigid grip.

Circling a row of farming equipment, she spied multiple figures hiding in the darkness. A shadowy figure moved toward Sue and Blake's position, using the shadows for cover. Dark eyes focused on a small length of broken wood. She snatched it up and threw it with all her strength. The missile sailed true, smacking the assailant in the back of the head. He collapsed and rolled into the waiting ocean.

"Damn it, they're behind us," a shooter screamed. He turned spraying the area with automatic fire.

Amazona ducked behind a small tractor, letting the metal shield take the damage. Her fingers closed on the thick undercarriage. She lifted it above her head like a plaything and hurled it at the shooters.

"Oh hell," A wailing scream accompanied the crash. "It's time to get out of here." The rush of footsteps sounded in the darkness.

"What about our money?"

"We can't spend it in the jug."

Red flashes came from the boats, as they neared the ladders leading to the topside of the docks. Wood chips floated in the churning water. "I wonder how they would like this?" Amazona mumbled, she jerked a heavy crate above her head.

It splashed in the water near the lead boat, drenching the men inside. The small craft lurched wildly to the side. The fire from Blake and Sue's position had stopped. A wave of panic tingled up her spine; her hands closed on a wide plow and sent it flying.

It crashed in the center of the boat, snapping it in half. Shouted curses and the screams of the injured filled the night. The second boat stopped. The bright light winked out. After several seconds it turned and departed. The engine sounds grew fainter.

"Blake," she shouted, her bare feet smacking the rough cut timbers. "Are you alright?"

"Yeah, I'm fine." He slowly rose to his feet. "Looks like you saved my bacon again."

She ran into his arms, lifted him in the air. With a sense of urgency her lips found his. "Thank God, you're okay."

"Thanks for asking, but I'm okay too," Sue snapped. "We need to hurry. The Moon Man may need our help."

The Moon Man rolled to his right. He rose to one knee. The automatic moved like an extension of his arm. He didn't notice the recoil as two slugs perforated the hood's belly. The pistol locked open. He depressed the release. The empty magazine tumbled to the ground. He quickly stuffed another inside.

Pain erupted in the Moon Man's leg; he crumpled on the trash covered floor. "You thought you killed me the other night." Slingshot McGuire, his torso wrapped in stained bandages, shuffled into the huge room. "I managed to escape and get back here. They brought a German sawbones in to take care of me. Didn't care much for his bedside manner. Doubt if I'll live through this, but I'll be famous as the guy who killed the Moon Man." His arm lifted slowly, the large pistol heavy in his hand centered on the masked man's chest.

The Moon Man scanned the floor searching for his lost pistol. He spotted the checked grip under the stack of lumber. *Talk about a longshot.* He licked his lips nervously, preparing to leap as McGuire stepped forward. The masked man stopped at the edge of the pile of discarded 2X4's.

"I want you to suffer. I'm gonna blast your kneecaps out first." His finger closed on the trigger.

The cloak fluttered behind him as he dropped to the floor. Gloved hands caught the end of a board perched atop the stack. His weight drove the free end up into the thug's hand, tipping the barrel upward. The bullet smacked the ceiling and dropped to the floor.

"Damn you," Slingshot screamed. Fresh blood dotted the bandage, as he strained against the weight of the pistol, trying to line up a second shot.

The Moon Man came to his feet, the .38 gripped in his fist. "Don't try it. I'll kill you."

Slingshot hesitated for a moment. "I've got nothing to lose?" He shifted the automatic toward the masked man.

Two dark red stains blossomed on McGuire's chest, spreading quickly to his stomach. Slingshot fell to his knees spitting blood. "Damn you, Moon Man. I'll see you in hell." He dropped to the floor.

Wearily, the Moon Man collected his weapons and limped into the darkness.

A small group escorted Amazona and Blake Manners to the train station three days later.

"You're telling me the Moon Man saved your life?" Gil McEwen shook his head in disbelief.

"He did," Amazona nodded. "If not for him Madame Terror and the Veiled Lady would have killed us all."

"It's a shame those two got away." Detective Sergeant Stephen Thatcher mumbled. He glanced over his shoulder to Sue McEwen as she pushed his wheelchair.

"Settle down big boy, you should still be in the hospital." She turned to her father. "See, Dad, the Moon Man isn't all bad."

"He's a crook, just like all the others in this town." Gil shook his head. "The only difference is he wears a fishbowl on his head."

Amazona smiled sweetly, as she stepped close to the detective. "If you see the Moon Man, thank him for me." Her wide stretched arms drew Sue to her chest. She released her after several seconds. "Take good care of him." She met Sue's eyes. "This is a good man you have."

"I know." Sue returned her wide smile, her hand closed on Stephen's arm.

"Come on, Zona. We've got to get back to California. Chambers is anxious for the story." He tugged her away from Stephen and Sue. "It'll be in all the papers, Lieutenant. I think I'll call it The Moon Man, Defender of Great City." He nodded. His hand clasped Amazona's, as they walked to the train.

"The Defender of Great City, You've got to be kidding me." Gil yanked his hat from his head, slamming it to the ground. "He's nothing but a hood."

"I'm not sure, Gil. He stuck around until the other cops arrived before he disappeared." Stephen patted Sue's hand.

"Don't you go getting soft on me," Gil shouted. "That bum ain't a hero." The Lieutenant met his daughter's eyes. "Get him home, Sue. He needs to heal up before he returns to duty."

THE END

WHO IS AMAZONA, THE MIGHTY WOMAN

Most pulp fans know about The Moon Man. Created by Frederick C. Davis, he is a Robin Hood type character that steals from the criminal and gives the money to the people in need in the fictional Great City. He's not a top tier character like Doc Savage, The Shadow, or The Spider, but he is a very good second or third tier character. He has a fiancé Sue McEwen and Ned Dargan as well as associates that would like to see the Moon Man in prison such as Sue's father Gil. The character was in 38 adventures in Ten Detective Aces magazine, the final adventure being "The Whitejack Jury" in January of 1937. When I read my first Moon Man adventure, I really liked the character and wondered where the idea for Mysterio's mask came from in the Spider-Man comics.

I discovered Amazona when I was doing research for a story and was looking at the Public Domain Superheroes website. The character fascinated me. Amazona made her only comic book appearance in the third issue of Planet Comics published by Fiction House in May of 1940. William Locke is credited with creating the character and Alex Blum and Dan Zolnerowich are credited with the artwork.

A woman of unmatched strength and beauty, she survives in the arctic with the last members of a super race of humans that nearly perished in the last ice age. Reporter Blake Manners accidently finds their arctic citadel after an unsuccessful arctic expedition in which he is the only survivor after his boat becomes ice bound. She falls in love with the American reporter at first sight and accompanies him to the United States after she frees his ship from the ice.

Once they arrive stateside, they attend a party which is crashed by a bunch of gangsters intent on robbing everyone attending the event. Amazona is the only heroine to battle a gang of thieves wearing a red dress and high heels. She makes short work of the criminals and avoids dying in a car explosion at the end of the story. The blurb at the end promised another adventure with Blake and Amazona where she helps him track down a murderer, alas the story never happened.

She has super strength—in one scene in the comic she lifts a car above her head—Superhuman endurance, cat-like agility and immunity from the cold, she's running around the arctic in a unitard. Many people think that Amazona was based on Wonder Woman, but in fact she pre-dates the Amazon Princess by over a year as Wonder Woman saw print late in 1941. Makes you wonder what Dr. Marston was reading before he created his famous character. Perhaps if Fiction House had published more adventures of The Mighty Woman, she might have evolved over time and still be in print today.

The team up between these two very different characters seemed natural to me. They could very easily mix in the other's world. The time frame for this adventure would be roughly early to mid 1940. People in America were concerned and scared, some were frightened of Hitler and what he was doing in Europe and some were afraid of the American Nazi party and the rallies they were having in the large metropolitan areas. This made a perfect time period to tell this story.

TERRY ALEXANDER - and his wife Phyllis live on a small farm near Porum, Oklahoma. They have three children and ten grandchildren. Terry is a member of the Oklahoma Writers Federation, Ozark Writers League, The Tahlequah Writers and The Fictioneers. He has been published in various anthologies from Airship 27, Pro Se Press, Metahuman Press, Pulp Modern, Hazardous Press, May December Press, to name a few.

THE ROBIN HOOD OF THE PULPS

THE ROBIN HOOD OF THE 1930'S RETURNS!

Detective Sgt. Stephen Thatcher is the son of Police Chief Peter Thatcher. Sickened by the effects of the Great Depression on Great City, the young lawman cannot reconcile the rich society elite living the good life while across town the poor of Great City go hungry. Unable to correct this injustice through the system he represents, Thatcher assumes the role of the vigilante thief the Moon Man by disguising himself behind a one-way Argus glass globe. In this get up he then proceed to rob the rich and give to the needy via his loyal aide, former boxer Ned "Angel" Dargan. He is also aided by the lovely Sue McEwen, the daughter of the man sworn to capture him, his own boss, Lt. Detective Gil McEwen.

Created by pulp legend Frederick C. Davis, the Moon Man's exploits appeared in the pages of "Ten Detective Aces" and was a reader favorite. Now he returns to the streets of Great City in five new thrilling adventures written by writers Ken Janssens, Gary Lovisi, Erwin K.Roberts and Andrew Salmon. Pulpdom's most bizarre hero is back on the case with a cover by Rob Davis & Rich Woodall as well as twelve interior illustrations by Ralf Van Der Hoeven.

AN AIRSHIP 27 PRODUCTION

NEW PULP

PULP FICTION FOR A NEW GENERATION!
CHECK AVAILABILITY AT: AIRSHIP27HANGAR.COM

During the golden days of American pulps hundreds of masked avengers were created to battle evildoers around the globe. *The Black Bat, Moon Man, Domino Lady*, and the *Purple Scar* to name only a few of these amazing pulp heroes. Now in each all-new volume New Pulp writers introduce to pulp readers brand new pulp heroes cast in the mold of their 1930s counterparts.

In each volume of *Mystery Men & Women* find a collection brand new action-packed stories starring original heroes to thrill and excite pulp fans everywhere as brought to you by Airship 27 Productions.

www.ingramcontent.com/pod-product-compliance
Lightning Source LLC
Chambersburg PA
CBHW051128260626
47170CB00005B/1711